INNER UNIVERSE

Copyright © 2021 by Tom Millar

Translated by Anna Galt (www.drama-panorama.com)

First paperback edition February 2022

Book design by Dania Zafar, Sonja Langewald, Saad Matze Himel

Map by Chaim Halter (chaimholtjer.com)

Co-creation: Dirk Brueckner

ISBN 978-1-7399292-0-6 (paperback)

ISBN 978-1-7399292-1-3 (ebook)

www.theinneruniverse.com

INNER UNIVERSE

SURPRISES FROM WITHIN

An Extraordinary Journey to an
Unknown Familiar World

TOM MILLAR

Translated by Anna Galt

DEDICATION

For all beings on this earth.
May they be healthy.
May they be happy.
May they be at peace.

CONTENTS

The Inner Universe
N
W
E
S
Factory
Formations
Market
Archive
The gate of Potential
garden Fields
Entertainment
Main Road
Tower
West-end Main Houses
Castle
Parliament
Senate
The main Gate
The outer World of form

PROLOGUE

You normally begin a preface with all kinds of personal things. A few acknowledgements perhaps, and a few words to explain what follows, so that you, dear reader, know what you're in for. But this is going to be different. I'd like to start the foreword with an experiment – with a short story.

What is it about?
Well, somehow it's about a person reading a book. And somehow it's not.

What kind of book, you ask?
This book. I don't know.

But see for yourself what happens.
Have fun reading.

Do it and see

Not even ten minutes in, she's laughing out loud. At the same time, a third car is running over her phone. She doesn't even notice. She turns the pages quickly and wishes she had a coffee. That's the downside to the parking lot here at the beach – no coffee. The freedom of being single makes you hungry in no time. Just three hours and a bit into this situation and she already needs food.

Her first chicken curry in ten years. He would be so shocked to see her eat meat. She smiles with satisfaction and goes back to pick up the remains of her phone. Later that day she carefully buries the shattered pieces and holds a little funeral ceremony she makes up on the spot. The speech is moving and the grave looks really beautiful with a yellow iris on it.

The new may come after a cycle has been completed, she says to herself, holding her hands at her heart. Destruction is a good thing, sometimes.

Three days later and halfway through the book, tears are running down her cheeks. The coffee next to her on the bench has turned cold, while her head feels hot. "The new begins in an empty space," she remembers her teacher in India saying. "Why me, and why again?" she asks the boxes piled up high in the front yard of the place she has called home for some time.

"So glad you came." She hugs her friend before starting to load the boxes.

The new place is furnished and after her third glass of wine, she relaxes a bit and continues reading the book. Can't be wrong to take a look, can it? Let's see who's on duty. Is there anyone judging? Who's angry? What is that...?

She wakes up frightened. What a dream. What a nightmare. What a release – it was only a dream. She almost enjoys the feeling, but then reality hits as she opens her eyes. Shuddering waves of happiness surge through her body, leaving a tickling sensation around her first chakra. Is that something new emerging? Is that the new excitement after all that yelling, screaming, crying, hoping when they were still together? It's quiet now, much quieter than she hoped for.

Row 23, Seat A – the window seat. Clouds outside. Excitement mounts as she opens the book again. Three more hours and then sunshine, mostly, for the next few months. That tingling feeling flashes up inside her again, brought on by that mental image.

Perfectly timed, right before her first yoga class starts, she turns the last page of the book. And with a new smile on her face she walks into the shala, surrounded by jungle filled with singing birds. As she folds her hands to begin the yoga session, a new chapter begins.

Down by the beach someone passes the bench she was sitting on before and notices a book. He sits down, and not even ten minutes in, he's laughing out loud.

PART I

A LOOK AT EVERYDAY LIFE

CHAPTER 1

Before It All Began

Stuck on repeat

I'm hanging out with my old friend Eric again. We're sipping coffee, talking about yoga. Well actually, we're talking about the lack of women in my life. He thinks I subconsciously avoid women. What a load of rubbish. It's just not easy to meet new people at the moment. Clubs? Looks like those times are gone. Also, it seems highly unlikely that I'd find someone to have a genuine conversation with in a club. "Ah, you like rock climbing? Tell me more!" I shout, while she screams the details of her last climbing trip into my right ear. Thanks, but no thanks.

Eric has known about my dilemma for a while and understands the gravity of the situation. One of his solutions is: do yoga! I'm not sure why he suggests this, since he's well aware of my thoughts on that half-naked stretching orgy. Just the other day, I saw a poster advertising Acroyoga: "Let your souls dance together." According to the picture, I'm supposed to balance a woman on my feet and make her feel like she's flying. In my case, a complete stranger – absolutely insane! And now Eric's going on at me about it too.

"I don't go to a ballet class just because I want to dance and meet people."

"Meet women! To be precise," Eric corrects me. "Why do you get so angry when we talk about this?"

"I'm not angry." I look at him in surprise.

Eric doesn't say anything. I take a big gulp of coffee. I miss my mouth and some of it lands in an unfortunate place on my pants. "Let's change the subject."

"I think you should go to the workshop."

"That's not what I meant when I said let's change the subject," I respond, scratching the back of my head again. I go to take another sip of my coffee, but the cup is empty. Time to order a second latte.

"I feel like the workshop could make a real difference."

"You and your mysterious prophecies. Is that some spiritual weakness of yours?"

We both laugh and do end up changing the subject. Now we're talking about shamanism. The things Eric knows are absolutely fascinating. My own shamanic journey comes back to mind. I had completely forgotten what it feels like, although I love exploring fantasy worlds.

"So how do I find my spirit animal?" I ask. "Wait, and what are animal guides? This other world seems to have more animals than the zoo!" My flippant comment doesn't sit well with the master. Still, Eric patiently explains what the animals stand for and how the different metaphors can act as guides. As I said, fascinating.

Later, on my way home, I can't seem to forget one of Eric's comments. He cleverly slipped "Do it, Tom" into our goodbyes. I arrive home and by chance pick up one of those flyers Eric always leaves lying around when he visits. "Navigate your emotions," the bright, bold letters instruct.

I'd love to be as relaxed and self-confident as Eric when it comes to feelings and women, but his slim, athletic figure makes it so much easier for him. Me, on the other hand… plus all the sweating. "How could it possibly work?" I ask myself in the mirror, shaking my head. I haven't gotten close enough to a woman recently to even be rejected.

My reflection speaks to me, now quite insistently: "Tom, something has to change, urgently."

"But what?" I reply. I go back to the kitchen to see what my fridge has in store for dinner. I'll skip the beer this time. I set the table with the usual butter-cheese-lettuce ensemble and pull some bread rolls out of my backpack. Netflix keeps me company as a bowl of chocolate pudding vanishes for dessert. Two, if I'm honest.

Two days later, I'm not sure how much voodoo magic Eric was really using on me. He swears he has nothing to do with the fact that I'm holding a booking confirmation for a four-day workshop in southern Germany in my hands. The fact that the map has transferred itself onto my shirt because of my sweating shows how serious the situation is. The description talks about four fundamental emotions that will be dealt with in the workshop, and about attachment to and judgement of them. Are fits of anger getting legitimised now?

Further down the workshop description, it says: "Invite your tears." I'm starting to sweat again, and I briefly wonder if maybe my drops of sweat are really tears in another form. Thankfully, I have to go out, which means I can put the question and the workshop brochure aside with a clean conscience for now, change my shirt, and leave the apartment.

Manú's life

"And send," she whispers to herself. Then she smiles and contentedly closes her laptop. She slips on her shoes, shoves the yoga mat into her backpack, and slams the door behind her. The sound of the quick rhythm of her steps in the staircase soon fades away.

The yoga sequence is going extraordinarily well today. Without a doubt, today's going to be a good day, Manú decides after her shower. And it is, as she confirms to her friend that evening, when they're sitting comfortably in the rooftop cafe Klunkerkranich.

"I did it," Manú says finally.

"Did what?"

"I booked the workshop about emotions." Manú beams at her friend, full of anticipation.

Her friend widens her eyes and says: "Are you sure you're ready?"

"Yes, I am. – Well, I think so."

She still seems skeptical. Then she leans over to Manú, gives her a quick hug and says: "I really hope you enjoy it. Fingers crossed for your exploration of emotions."

"Shame you can't come."

"I guess the universe wants you to go alone."

"Don't be silly," laughs Manú, who always dismisses any spiritual mysticism that goes a bit overboard.

She immediately thinks of the yoga teacher she knew who preached compassion, but decided to 'practice asanas' with another woman. It wasn't enough that she fell for a total macho. No, it had to be a fake guru, as Manú's friend had called him. Do normal men even exist? Still no answer to that question.

"I just really want to get Patrick out of my system. And I want to meet some new people."

"Denial, my darling?" warns her friend. "You're still not over him, are you?"

Manú looks into her almost empty glass. "Why do I always meet these idiots? I probably have some cryptic invitation for these guys printed on my forehead."

They both laugh and her friend examines her forehead more closely. "Ah, yes, I see something here," she says. "Smart and funny. What's not to like?"

"Maybe there's just too many of them and the probability is just very high?" Manú asks her friend.

"Who knows, maybe you just have to adjust your idiot alarm system?"

The friend raises her glass. "Here's to only true heroes coming to this emotions workshop."

"Ha. But the next knight in shining armour will definitely have to prove his honour before he's allowed to take his armour off."

"The poor guy, I already feel sorry for him."

They end the evening laughing. Life feels good. "An excellent day today," she confirms to her reflection as she brushes her teeth. And on top of that, she'll be traveling to southern Germany to learn how to navigate her emotions soon. In the meantime, she enjoys her life in Berlin, although every once in a while, she dreams of a life in a community in the countryside, away from all the hustle and bustle and sensory overload of a big city.

CHAPTER 2

Once Upon a Time

A small kitchen, somewhere in southern Germany

I'm peeling carrots. Lunch is supposed to be served in 45 minutes, so everyone in the little kitchen of the seminar centre is rushing around. Four people are cutting, chopping, and stirring – and giving everything a final taste.

In the midst of all this, there's a wide-legged pair of pink and blue trousers, suitable for meditating in, dancing to and fro along with their owner's swift movements. She's also wearing a yellow T-shirt that reads: "It's never wrong to do the right thing." The young woman is providing us with an amusing commentary on the proceedings in the kitchen. This encourages me to drop a quip in here and there. Over time, a conversation that'd be worthy of the stage develops. If only we weren't pressured for time to get lunch on the table.

"I'd be very grapeful if you'd be so kind as to pass me the cucumber."

"Very well, but lettuce not forget the tomatoes."

"What an egg-cellent thought! I'd appreciate it berry much if you'd stir the sauce for a second."

"Ah, yes, but let me ketchup on chopping the parsley first."

"Orange you glad we're almost done here?"

"I've never bean this hungry before."

The jokes keep flying.

Lunch is served and after a short break, we're all back in the workshop room ready for the next exercise. Everyone searches for a partner. I end up with a guy called Walter. We start cursing loudly at each other. At first, I find it pretty funny, but then my partner insults me so severely that I start to actually feel a bit angry. I force myself to react with a bit more gusto, but the feeling of embarrassment at being actually hurt holds me back. I also find it quite silly, screaming around the place like this for no reason. My partner seems to be made for it, because he's really getting himself worked up into a fit of rage, and my comparatively mild comebacks only seem to encourage him: "You think that's funny, asshole?!"

I'm just about to really get going, because "asshole" crosses a line, but our workshop leader stops us and asks for absolute silence. Now we're supposed to express the energy of anger in a dance. A shiver runs down my back. I'm actually only really angry at Eric, who had a big hand in me ending up in this situation. I move somewhat mechanically and fight the urge to just leave the room.

The woman from the kitchen dances freely,

unselfconsciously. Incredibly, it actually even looks good. I don't want to know what I must look like. The amount I'm sweating fits more to her dance than mine.

Eric would say this experience is expanding my horizons, I suddenly think.

I still have two days to go. I'm relieved when the music stops. I haven't looked forward to a fifteen-minute meditation this much in a long time. We're supposed to sense the feelings we just felt and appreciate them. For the first five minutes, all I feel is sweat running down my body, then everything calms down, and so do I.

My gaze drifts outside. What was once a farm has been transformed into a workshop venue and guest house with a little community garden, a cat, 26 chickens, and seven ducks – none of which are intended for slaughter. There are people too, of course – twelve individuals who work together to cultivate clarity and humanity. It really impresses me.

I remember a visit to this community last year. It was Eric who brought me here of course. So I'm familiar with the place, where shared resources, open conversations, and an otherwise rarely encountered culture of appreciation are commonplace. I feel comfortable in this kind of environment. But I am skeptical when it comes to overly interdependent decision-making and how the community's interest very much determines your everyday life.

The exercise in the workshop room is coming to an end. I've been able to show my anger more than I expected – "made space for my inner rage to scream" – as the workshop facilitator would say. I feel good, no, I feel great, and I'm excited for what's to come.

All of this leaves me exhausted at the end of the day. The desire to withdraw to my shared room, which I chose for budget reasons, hits me early. When I go up the stairs to the first floor of the guest house, I see the woman from the kitchen standing there.

"Hitting the hay?" she asks unexpectedly. She catches me off guard – I was still thinking about what to say to her.

"Yes, definitely. And you?"

"I'm going to read a bit first to wind down."

My brain is still trying to figure out what to ask her next. She didn't mention where she's from during the introduction circle, did she?

"Well, good night. Sleep well." She looks at me and then disappears into one of the few single bedrooms.

What's her name? Has she gone to other workshops like this? Who is her T-shirt quoting? Now the questions don't stop coming.

The sound of snoring coming from my room reminds me to take a short detour back to my washbag in the bathroom down the hallway. Equipped with my earplugs, I'm ready for an adventure in the world of dreams.

But a single bedroom doesn't prevent restless sleep and intense dreams either, as my new acquaintance confirms the next morning. At seven o'clock sharp, all of us gather for the morning meditation. Then some exercises barefoot in the dewy grass, followed by breakfast. The bland, slimy, textureless substance on my plate is actually called gruel. Buddha pushed his suffering to the limit to gain self-awareness. Jesus suffered, not only on the cross, but also in quite earthly situations. Strange thoughts this morning, but they somehow help me to face the gruel with some acceptance and to look forward to the day ahead.

As I will later find out, my new acquaintance – I really have to find out her name soon – feels similarly about the gruel. But first we're already onto the next topic of our workshop: sadness. The first exercise is to 'hold' my energetic centre at my core. The core is located right below the belly button as the facilitator Josua demonstrates by casually showing us his six-pack. We're supposed to imagine an object that represents our energetic centre. I choose a mango.

When some of the female workshop participants show admiration for his six-pack by looking dreamily at him, are they giving their 'centres' to this attractive guy? To learn to recognise these shifts of our centres in future, we're supposed to practice in pairs. Achim, not entirely the partner I would have chosen, is supposed to do all kinds of silly things, while I make sure that my centre stays below the navel.

My partner clumsily makes a fool of himself in front of me. It doesn't impress me much and I manage to keep my attention on the mango. The fact that his cheap cologne stinks up half the room, on the other hand, is really annoying me and soon I can't think about anything else. Maybe I let my 'centre' slip away. At least, that's what I suspect if I understood Josua correctly.

I'm glad when it's time for a break and I go outside. When I come back, my new acquaintance is standing at the door of the workshop room.

"What was your name again?" I ask and take a big sip of water from a full glass.

"Manú. And you, Tom?"

I inhale deeply and exhale with a laugh without falling for her little trick. However, this surprise attack suddenly erases all the other questions I had at the ready. "Did you understand the centre exercise?" I ask, after what seems an eternity.

"Yes."

Then it's time to go back to the workshop and the stream of other participants gently pushes us back into the room. I finish my water and sit down.

"Invite your tears to come," Josua begins the meditation with his soft and wistful voice. It's quiet and I start sweating.

"A child happily dancing on the grass. Is that your father, looking on so happily?" You could hear a pin drop in the room.

"It's the love that lives inside of you. A child's laugh – follow it. Do you see the child standing in the grass? Go there and take them by the hand."

Next to me, I notice a quiet sob. I take a deep breath in and hold it in; my heart starts beating louder. Sitting in this position is starting to get uncomfortable too and I can't get the image of my dad out of my head. He's wearing that shirt, the one where he always rolled up his sleeves.

Yes, he's laughing. My throat is dry and I try yet again to find a more comfortable seated position.

Then I hear Josua say: "It's you, that laughter behind those walls. Where you can smell the flowers blooming on the meadow. Imagine your tears melting those walls. Brick by brick, with every tear, the walls dissolve..."

Once Walter starts crying and the other men follow, I get incredibly hot. Happy for an excuse to leave, I suddenly feel the urge to use the bathroom. I stand up silently and creep out of the room. The fresh breeze that comes through the bathroom window cools me down. Three of the seven ducks seem to be looking at me from the garden. I would love to run around the house as carelessly.

I take a deep breath and, with slight dread, know that I should go back in now.

Inside, everyone is hugging each other. My first impulse to turn around immediately is nipped in the bud by Josua, who gently, yet firmly pulls me back into the circle. Arms start wrapping around my shoulders from all sides and I try to stare at a spot on the floor. The violin music, which the entire group is swaying to, even causes my eyes to fill with a few tears in the end.

I'm confused, because no one seems put off by each other's tears. But I'm still happy when the workshop is over.

The rest of the afternoon is more relaxed. In the evening, we sit around the fire and talk about life. Josua joins with his guitar and starts to play. Oh no, now I have to sing?! He asks the group if anyone would like to sing a song. I yawn for the third time in a row. My eyes are burning slightly and I don't know any songs. But it was still a lovely evening. Tired and a little drowsy, I fall into bed.

On Sunday, the workshop continues on a more cheerful note. We celebrate joy. In the afternoon, we clean and polish the whole place, and then Josua closes the workshop with a heartfelt thank you.

"We've truly emotionally connected with each other in the past few days. Some of you have experienced changes in surprising ways. And I'm sure I can speak for everyone when I say you got to know yourselves a little better. That feeds the soul and shows me what we are all capable of if we are brave enough."

His closing remarks leave me incredibly proud. I really did it. I got through the workshop. I could hug the entire world, I feel full of strength and happiness. This seems to be a new feeling. Wow.

I stay on the farm for a few extra days and enthusiastically lend a helping hand to the community. I especially enjoy the sustainable agriculture and the delicious, fresh vegetables we eat. Talking to people here is kind of extraordinary. They're different somehow. I feel comfortable and I'm in a good mood. The intense way people seem to stare at you when talking does take a bit of getting used to though. If I did that in Berlin, I'd probably get some snarky comment.

The witty young woman with the kind of spiritual outfit stays too. We work together in the garden, where our conversation gets a bit deeper. But I still have to overcome one reappearing hurdle – thanks to my insufficient interest in names, I've forgotten it again. No matter how hard I try, I just can't remember it. Finally, another cooking session gives me a chance.

"I know this might sound strange, but can you tell me your name again? I kind of forgot it, sorry."

As I stammer these words, it becomes clear that the myth of women's gift for multi-tasking doesn't hold up in practice. Completely immersed in the spicy flavor of a soup, she says, "Em…" (pause), "Manú" (another pause).

"Is that it?" I ask.

"Well, it's not like you're going to remember much more!" She looks at me amused with her dark brown eyes. It seems she was able to abruptly refocus her attention away from the soup tasting and catch me off guard with this quip.

"These gaps almost always come after a moment of surprise," explains a tall fellow chef. "In a perceptual vacuum like that, I could, for example, drink your last sip of coffee and you wouldn't even notice."

"So let me recap: We now know that my name is 'Em Manú' and yours is 'Tom'. Was that formulated appropriately for your male brain?" Manú asks curiously.

"I bet we could renovate half the kitchen in the time it takes you to recover from your 'moment' of surprise," she continues.

"Is that your observation?" the tall chef softly asks Manú. The response is silence and then the kitchen crew enters the dining area. Determined not to give this Manú the field without some sort of comeback, I follow the group to a table. She smiles reassuringly, as we sit down. Okay, forget it.

The next day, we're busy gardening again. We're both happy to talk about the workshop we just did, because Manú doesn't quite get some of the terminology and ideas either. Four fundamental emotions, an energetic centre and a 'gremlin' that represents the selfish behavior of our egos.

Anyway, we realise that somehow it's always about some energy we're supposed to perceive in ourselves. I've heard about this many times before. Buddhism is about energies, my father taught me that. yoga is too, as Manú explains to me. There are energy centres called chakras. But bad vibes and good vibes? I have to pass on that.

"Well, have you never been to a party you really enjoyed because you got along with most of the people there?" Manú asks.

"I remember an event recently where I made an escape plan fifteen minutes into it, because of the people."

"Those are bad vibes, or you can call it oscillatory instability if you want to get really scientific."

"So are we experiencing good vibes right now?" I ask.

"I hope so." Manú blinks because of the sun in her eyes and hops over to the lettuce.

"You should put on some sunscreen, your face is pretty red already."

I nod. "Yes, thanks." But I'm not really sure whether it's the sun or my question about the good vibes that's making me turn red.

During dinner, the subject of energy comes up again. This time, however, we discuss alternative energy production using a locally operated kinetic power plant. Air-filled hollow chambers are connected one after another, if I understand correctly.

"And how does the power generation work then?" I ask the group.

"A vertical pipe is filled with water and has floating containers on a conveyor belt inside," explains a smaller, bearded resident, who must be over 60 – at least. His eyes shine with enthusiasm, like someone discovering the world for the first time.

"The containers fill up with water on their way to the bottom of the pipe. Then water gets pumped out of the containers at the bottom of the pipe and the buoyancy forces them upwards. This drives a generator and in the end we have enough energy for our entire farm here." Opinions and ideas for implementing such a project are exchanged back and forth. I find it challenging to keep up.

My thoughts stray a little when the specialist discussion goes beyond what I can follow and I remember our conversation in the garden, when Manú explained good and bad vibes to me. That was also about energy. Could the production of sustainable energy be similar to good vibes? I ask myself. And what about the chakras? Is that the same as electricity?

"Hello, Major Tom. Are you receiving?"

I'm mildly startled. "Yeah, everything's fine." I look at their grinning faces.

"A daydream?" Jolina asks. Her long, dark hair reveals some of the mandala-like tattoos on her strong shoulders.

"Maybe," I answer, still not entirely present.

"Follow your train of thought. It could be important," she adds a little mysteriously before the conversation turns back to the gardening work that has been done.

A little later, I'm in my bed. Random thoughts about the energies inside me and out there keep me awake for a while. The feeling of being in a good mood and the idea of 'good vibes' is the last thing I can remember when I am woken up by a conscientious rooster the next morning. Its crow resounds repeatedly throughout the farm.

It wins. At 6:20, I get up. I grab a cup of coffee from the kitchen and go outside. Dew on the grass reflects the low-standing sun in countless glittering jewels. Two bees are busy flying from flower to flower during their morning shift. A cat patrols the vegetable garden. Then my eyes take in the unbelievable alpine panorama opening up on the horizon for the first time today. Wow. I take off my shoes and socks and walk through the dewy grass. Only gradually do the soles of my feet report a low temperature to my brain. They decide 'cold' and recommend 'dryness and warmth'. All that fresh air and morning magic have given me an appetite. In a good mood, I set off for breakfast – fortunately, this time without gruel.

After a delicious morning meal, I pack my things. Soon after, my rental car, containing two melancholy looking people, backs out of the driveway. Manú is from Berlin too, so we've decided to drive back together.

On the way, we decide that there's definitely quite a lot of ambiguity to the concept of energy, but our conversation doesn't go much deeper than that. The grey-blue colours of the German autobahn must make passengers sleepy, because Manú's eyes fall shut from time to time. Maybe the kind of intense days at the workshop are also partly to blame.

The signs for Berlin start to show double digits and I've gone through at least five variations by now: How can I ask Manú if we can see each other again?

When she suddenly wakes up, I seize the moderately good opportunity: "Manú, I have a question."

She stretches, looks at me, and says: "Go ahead."

Suddenly the brilliant formulation disappears from my head and I'm left with: "We have a lot to talk about, you know, personal development and spirituality."

"Okay," Manú replies.

I feel like I've played myself into a corner. At least that's what I think when I feel a certain heat creeping up inside of me.

"Well, we've talked about energy. Don't you think it's strange that completely different things like chakras and power plants use the exact same word?"

"Yeah, it's crazy how many metaphors are used in spirituality. I feel like sometimes people have no idea what they're talking about." Manú looks ahead at the road and then gazes out the passenger window.

"How about we clarify things a bit, maybe over breakfast?" Now she looks at me as I wait anxiously for her reaction.

"Okay, let's serve the spiritual and scientific worlds and clarify the subject of energy," she says in a heroic tone. I'm not quite sure if that's a yes or a no. But then she laughs: "Sure, I'd love to. I look forward to it."

Joy rushes through my system, much like a long-awaited 1:0 in a football stadium.

"A sort of continuation of our mealtime talks at the farm. And we can eat that spread I brought with me," I add.

"Won-der-ful! I'm up for it as soon as you are."

The second Mexican wave rushes through my system as I take the exit towards Friedrichshain. I'm satisfied with myself, the workshop and the drive back to the big city. Eric once talked about a spiritual high that can occur after intense workshops like these. I think I know what he means now.

However, I didn't know anything about the spiritual hangover that it would turn into in the next two days. I'm familiar with its big brother, which you sometimes bring home as a souvenir from a night out, but not with so much heaviness, lethargy, and doubt. Eric gladly helps me out of this mood. Since I'm still pretty anti-yoga, we go running, meditate in the forest, and he tells me a bit more about the widespread phenomenon of the spiritual hangover. "Acceptance has a lot to do with understanding," he says.

"Well, at least I feel much better now."

CHAPTER 3

Energy Here and Beyond

The first breakfast – and the first currents

It's a Saturday in May just like any other when the doorbell rings at number 80 Erich-Weinert-Strasse. The sign on the bell reads Manú S. Kaytoni. The door opens with a "Greetings, stranger." Manú has laid out a lavish spread. Coffee, cheese, and jam are waiting. I add the handmade spreads from the farm in southern Germany. Now everything's ready to be eaten with relish. Finally, I arrange the bread rolls and Manú immediately jumps in with the question: "So, what is energy?"

"I asked the internet for some help and did a bit of preparation," I tell her proudly.

"And, was it able to help?" enquires Manú.

"Yes, I had a little lightbulb moment actually."

"In what way?"

"A bit of heat, a few particles or waves, depending on the weather conditions. The rest falls under the 'I don't know' category, and then in the end, a light goes on."

"True, it's a little light," Manú says. "We should give it a bit of a boost."

"Coffee?" I try to keep the conversation going without dwelling too much on my limited knowledge of light. She nods and holds out her cup to me. I'm fascinated by the porcelain teapot, which reminds me of sophisticated English tea culture and somehow doesn't fit this apartment, which has clearly been put together DIY, but with love.

"We've already established that energy has something to do with electricity," Manú ponders. "Maybe it'd help to think about how electricity works first? Like I know that there's sometimes a plus or a minus and that it feels weird when I touch the wrong place."

"Yeah, but you can still get a shock even if you know how it works." I remember an incident when I was trying to wire up a light in my kitchen.

"In any case, it's a long story that begins in the 18th century with Benjamin Franklin and Alessandro Volta and continues into the 19th century with Nicola Tesla."

Manú's eyes open wide in feigned horror: "Maybe we should stick to energy itself a little more. Life is short, and history is long. I think we need to prioritise." She presses her lips together and nods her head several times.

What am I supposed to say to that? "Okay, then I'll fast forward." I make what I imagine to be fast-forwarding sounds. Manú laughs. This gives me time to put the fundamentals together in my head.

"Alternating current. The plus and minus poles switch

back and forth as fast as lightning. Fifty times a second, therefore 50 hertz."

Manú makes an astonished face as she sips her coffee.

"And still, we talk about plus and minus, or rather neutral conductors. Current flows from plus to minus, I learned that in school. But actually it's the other way around because the so-called free electrons move towards the positive pole in the current conductor."

"How are these electrons supposed to manage if the plus pole changes all the time?"

"Well, they don't even notice going the wrong way, because they just do what the dipole moment demands."

"So, what's the energy in electricity?" Manú asks.

"I wondered the same thing, just like science has, with one difference: they found answers."

"So? Did you copy some of their answers?"

"I did: energy use is only possible if two different energy levels exist. For example, if one part of the current conductor has 0 volts and another has 230. Then we have what's called potential."

"Amazing!" Manú exclaims. "Does that have anything to do with developing inner potential? Like we talked about in the workshop?" A small tomato disappears whole into her mouth and I'm not sure how seriously she's taking my explanation.

"So this potential is, let's say, a deliberate imbalance. Electrons are missing at this point of potential. There's a surplus of positive ones. That's what it takes to get the current flowing when you turn on the light. Do you get me?" I ask.

"Yeah, sure: I heard everything you said and I mostly understand." As she nods to emphasise what she just said, a strand of light brown hair sneaks out of her ponytail and falls over her eyes. She sweeps it back with her left hand and simultaneously brings the coffee cup to her mouth with her right hand. Phenomenal.

"This potential corresponds to potential energy. It can be converted into kinetic energy when the potential reaches the neutral pole, so when the circuit is closed. Electricity starts flowing when the electrons rush to the plus side, towards the +230V potential."

"I have one more question for you, professor: Why does the bulb light up when electrons go towards the plus?"

The professor is getting hot under the collar. Even if he expressed it differently, my friend Eric has occasionally criticised me in a similar way. But I have to say these things somehow, right? I'm confused and take a deep breath.

"Professor? Is it really that bad?"

"No, no, no," Manú reassures me. "It's all good. I'm just a bit sensitive when it comes to explanations. My mother was a teacher, her entire idea of parenting consisted of them."

"Oh, I'm sorry," I own up. "Then I hereby announce the imminent end of the conductor." To my satisfaction, this amuses Manú.

"The conductor (so the copper wire) is a bit like a well-developed road and the light bulb is a narrow path leading through a dense forest. There's an electron crowd on that narrow forest path now. The electrons rub against each other and the branches, which generates heat and light. If the glow is supported a little bit by a vacuum or certain gases, then we have a light bulb."

Manú is astounded: "How do you know all this?"

"TV is pretty educational, so is the internet. Like I said, I did my homework for our breakfast."

"What a good boy."

Almost in sync, we chew on our breakfast rolls as we let the information sink in. Later, we agree that there should be another energetic breakfast. The front door of number 80 Erich-Weinert-Strasse falls shut and I go home – touched, somehow.

The second breakfast and a quantum of amazement

I sit on the rather uncomfortable café chair and bump my knee against the crossbar of the stylish looking table for the second time. Who would design something like this? my internal commentator voice asks me. I don't know either, but luckily right then Manú comes through the door. She's wearing an orange top, blue denim shorts, and black flip-flops. Her hair is tied into a ponytail, which bounces from shoulder to shoulder as she walks.

"Wow, I'm hungry. And hello, first of all," is her bubbly greeting. For some unknown reason, I stand up. Manú looks at me somewhat puzzled and I explain clumsily: "Please sit down," pointing to the chair to my left.

She looks and says: "Sure, gladly. That's why I'm here."

What the hell was that about? my internal commentator asks reproachfully. I'd love to be a mole right now and burrow myself into the ground, but Manú asks if I've ever tried the matcha latte here. I haven't, so she promptly orders two from the waitress.

"You just have to try this!"

"Okay, I can't wait."

"And a large vegan breakfast," she calls after the waitress.

That idiot commentator takes over my actual voice and blurts out: "Me too!" Only then do I realise my beloved cheese has just been voted out of this breakfast. I have to regain control of my speech centre. Whoever that is speaking, go away!

Meanwhile, Manú begins: "I've looked up some stuff about quantum mechanics. What a fascinating tiny little world. Electricity seems to play a part there too somehow."

"How so?" I ask.

"I read that things in the quantum world work differently to the way they do in what they call the macro cosmos here all around us."

In the meantime, two matcha lattes have arrived, which surprisingly – to me at least – smell like cereal.

"So, what was the conclusion of your paper on quantum mechanics?" I ask, wondering whether Manú's going to play the professor too. A smile I obviously can't hide appears on my lips.

"What's so funny?" Manú asks immediately.

"Well, I just thought of the professor jibe the other day."

"And now you're wondering whether I can explain without sounding like one." I shrug and look at her briefly.

"Well then, may I have your attention as I present my semi-knowledge to serve the study of energy, without sounding like a professor."

I lean back and wait for the performance to start.

"Nineteenth century: the discovery of atoms. Not of hard matter, no, of soft consistency – doubts!"

I'm having some doubts of my own. Our vegan breakfast is being served and it looks completely different to what I imagined.

"Your attention please!" Manú raises her right hand, which is holding a grape from the vegan breakfast platter. She points at the grape: "This atom consists of an incredibly small, positively charged core – the nucleus, and a kind of shell, where the electrons we already know about are floating around."

"That's what I remember from school," I confirm.

"Well, here comes the surprise! The nucleus and the electrons are so much smaller than the atoms that we could easily say they're empty."

"Empty?"

"Imagine the atom has the radius of the city of Hamburg, and you're sitting in a café on the river Elbe. Your height would be approximately the size of the atomic nucleus, and somewhere in the city, a few bacteria are floating around. Those would be the electrons. At the same time, you represent more than 99% of the mass of the entire atom, meaning all of Hamburg."

"With or without coffee?" I ask.

"What?"

"Am I sitting there with coffee and cheesecake?"

"With coffee, but without cake."

"Too bad. I'm not available as a part of the model then."

"You're being silly and not paying attention!"

"I am," I protest, "and I like Hamburg as an example. I used to be an apprentice there."

"An apprentice in what?" asks Manú.

"To be a chef."

"Really? I couldn't tell when we were working in the kitchen in Bavaria."

"I wanted to fit in."

Manú rolls her eyes, which makes me a bit nervous.

"You can cook for me sometime. I'll gladly invite thirty friends and colleagues to eat à la carte. Does that inspire the master chef in you?" There's no way out, so I nod.

"Great," Manú responds, and my commentator voice adds a little "Well..."

"Where were we?" I deflect.

"With you as a possible atomic nucleus in Hamburg."

"Ah true, the cheesecake issue. For the record: I love cake. In any situation."

"Noted."

"So, Hamburg is almost empty while I sip my coffee by the river?"

"Exactly. And the shocking news isn't over. There are more particles in the nucleus: positively charged protons and neutral neutrons. These, in turn, are made of elementary particles, the quarks." For the last part, Manú pulls a little sheet of paper from her pocket and reads from it.

"As I said, absolutely shocking, since everybody believed in matter as the foundation of our world."

"And now?" I ask.

Manú swallows a hefty piece of avocado. "Now they think everything is energy. That's the reason I find it so fascinating. I learned about similar stuff in my yoga teacher training – the concept that we're all connected and that energy is the basis of the universe."

I'm amazed I've never heard about the similarity between these ideas before. I take a sip of matcha latte and finish the under-ripe fruit from my vegan breakfast platter. In the meantime, Manú has actually managed to reposition herself on her chair, which must be as uncomfortable as mine, with her left foot on her right thigh and vice versa.

"What are you doing?" I ask.

"Lotus position."

I'm so impressed I can't stop looking, which she notices, of course.

"If I understand correctly, what you're saying is that while these spiritual teachings explain it differently, they've always meant exactly what science has found out now through quantum physics?"

"Exactly. My yoga teacher always says, 'If there's something you want to know, search within yourself.' It's a method called awareness of the conscious mind."

Although I don't fully understand what Manú means, I

have the feeling that unlike many crackpot spiritual delusions, there seems to be a wisdom to this that should be taken seriously and can actually be scientifically proven.

"Yes, I get the same impression," Manú agrees.

"How do you know what I'm thinking?" I ask in surprise.

"Shot in the dark," she laughs.

"And you do this hatha yoga thing?" I ask with a mixture of horror and curiosity, and without really knowing what it is exactly.

"Basically, yes, but what I do is called Ashtanga yoga. It's a fixed sequence of exercises. How about you?"

"I haven't been able to talk myself into it."

"What's stopping you?"

"Well, maybe I find it too soft. Besides, I only know women who do yoga – this hatha thing."

"Well, why don't you try an hour of Ashtanga and find out for yourself if it's too soft?"

"I'll think about it," I answer half-heartedly. The idea of doing yoga with Manú – me not being able to do anything while she floats around in front of me like a feather – is the stuff of nightmares. I save myself by going back to our original subject and taking a big slurp of matcha latte. I take a deep breath to be on the safe side and then I start speaking without really knowing how it's all connected: "By employing the scientific methods so sacred to us, we've studied more and more details. For centuries we've walked the world with a torch and have found truths in the macro world, our everyday environment."

"What are you talking about?" asks Manú, puzzled.

"I'm not exactly sure either."

Manú laughs.

"Sorry, it's gone. I lost my train of thought."

"Now what?" asks Manú.

I don't know how to go on and I start feeling hot. An unfamiliar part of me suddenly says: "Tell me about this Ash...yoga."

"Ashtanga yoga?" Manú completes the word.

"Yes."

"When I get on the mat for my practice, it's an encounter with myself. I'm forced to listen to myself."

"What do you mean? Do you meditate on the yoga mat?" I ask.

"Actually, yoga is a preliminary stage of meditation. Especially for brainiacs like us, it helps to calm the mind. The mind is busy coordinating movements with breaths and it doesn't have time to think all over the place."

"I feel like yoga is a lot about posing. On social media, I only ever see athletic, flexible women in the most impossible contortions, smiling into the camera as if they were lazing around on the couch."

Manú rests her head on her hands as she thinks. This makes me nervous. Was I too harsh? I wasn't talking about her, just generally speaking. But it's the truth. The skintight outfits and positions that no average person can do.

Manú takes a deep breath and says, "You're absolutely right."

I'm surprised and don't know what to say. "Mmm," I hear myself respond.

"What you're talking about definitely exists. And whatever else you thought is probably true too."

I swallow audibly and absentmindedly reach for my glass of water. My throat feels dry.

"But even though it's true," she continues, "there might be other examples. Just as there might be people who have a strong opinion about something, say yoga, and then change their mind."

I can't think of a reply.

"I really wish more people would have the courage and willingness to practice yoga in the way it has been practiced for thousands of years."

"Which is?" I enquire, really curious now.

"It directs your attention inwards, towards yourself and your inner world. It doesn't even require the physical exercises. Funny, isn't it?" She pauses and then: "Just imagine that all this movement yoga doesn't even make up more than a tiny part of what people have been practicing in temples and far away from civilization in nature, for ages. Surrendering to the present moment, no matter what the outside world demands of you, that's what it's all about."

"Then why are there so many people doing all those exercises in specific outfits?"

Manú shrugs her shoulders. "Why do people drive fancy cars? Why do people shop in organic supermarkets? And what does knowledge mean to me? Isn't it usually about two things: function and prestige?"

"I never thought of it that way." A big grin appears on my face.

"What is it?" Manú wants to know.

"I'm not sure, but could it be that all these wise words have brought out Little Miss Professor after all?"

"Never!" Manú protests. She glances at me just to look away again and has a hard time containing her laughter.

I celebrate this rare win with a lovely sip of real coffee!

But once the vegan breakfast selection has been eaten, my triumph is forgotten. And then Manú actually does it: she convinces me to contort myself – Ashtanga-style – in a private yoga session next Saturday. Just thinking about it makes my body temperature go through the roof.

The third breakfast and invisible guidance

It's time to study energy a bit more. And so I once again find myself at the bakery ordering rolls, which I then carry to Erich-Weinert-Strasse. Manú has dutifully set the table again and very soon after I arrive, she begins: "The doubt that comes from quantum physics sometimes leads to incredible ideas. It even makes people question God, in the sense of a God with a beard sitting in heaven and judging humans from above."

"Aha."

"One of these ideas is that there's such a thing as super-luminal velocity." She looks at me expectantly.

"I have no idea what that means. And how did you get on to that?"

As if she had been waiting for this question, she

bombards me with more information. "The reason for a doubt like this is the phenomenon of entanglement. They experimented pulling apart quantum systems that belong together, so something like a quantum team. Part of the team was brought to a different place, but this didn't stop them behaving in sync with their other team members."

"So a team of synchronised swimmers," I throw in.

"Yes, a bit like that. Just that they were in different places, but still swimming perfectly synchronised."

Manú seems suddenly startled: "Was that too professory again?"

"A bit," I nod my head, "but it's interesting, what you're saying."

"Oh no, not again! Luckily, I'm done for now anyway," Manú assures, a little prematurely, because she immediately continues, "It's just an example of how science is slowly beginning to take the teachings of Eastern philosophies seriously. Western science often ends up at a dead end. That's disconcerting for them, but opens their minds to other alternatives."

Silence. The rolls on the table are untouched, but the coffee cups are almost empty.

"So religion doesn't seem entirely credible to you, as you insinuated with the bearded man in heaven. But even science constantly runs out of answers to questions about our existence. So what then?" I ask.

"Since there are so many unanswered questions, you can't just say, for example, that yoga is nonsense or sensing energy is hocus-pocus."

"I strongly object. I never said it like that."

"True," Manú admits. "Still, you seem to find it easier to believe a scientific expert who can provide facts and measurable data than a yogi who talks about consciousness."

"Also true."

"Well, there you go. Looks like we'll have to consult our own inner gurus. Coffee?" Manú arches her neck and peers into my empty cup.

"Coffee? Always yes." My gaze drifts into the distance.

"It thinks," comments Manú as she untangles her legs to go turn on the coffee machine. This suddenly reminds me of my first yoga lesson. "Where will the yogaing take place?" I casually enquire.

"Good question. Your place or mine?"

"Uh, your place. My apartment is too small."

"Okay. I have a second mat here, so all you have to bring is yourself in a pair of colourful leggings."

"Very funny," I mumble.

"I think so too," Manú cheekily agrees and screws the espresso machine together.

There are a few hiking pictures with, I assume, her friends, on the wall by the table. A couple of photos seem to be missing, given away by a thumbtack and some tiny remainders of paper.

"You like hiking?" I ask, looking at the pictures.

"Yes, that was with friends in Ireland, two years ago."

"Two pictures are missing," I note as neutrally as possible.

"That's right. They were past their sell-by dates."

I look puzzled and Manú concentrates on wiping an

imaginary spot on the perfectly clean countertop. I know better than to ask any more questions at this point.

Manú patiently and somehow absent-mindedly watches the espresso machine.

"I imagine it this way," she suddenly blurts out cheerfully as she pours me fresh coffee. "Buddha, Jesus, and a bunch of scientists are sitting around a table somewhere in the universe. There's a dim ceiling lamp. It's just enough to see how the universe as a whole works. There's a knock on the door and Einstein enters. He's carrying a shovel in one hand and a flashlight in the other. His face and hands are slightly dirty from digging in all the details.

"'Nice of you to finally join us,' says someone, who immediately gets a stern look from Buddha because of his comment. 'I've got it,' says Einstein and sits down. 'Everything is connected to everything, the universe is not absolute. And everything is based on energy.'

"'Chapeau,' say two scientists simultaneously – maybe Planck and Tesla – who are also sitting at the table. Einstein demonstratively puts his flashlight aside and adds with a smile: 'But I also know why.'

"'Yes, we've been working on it too,' says Planck. To which Buddha replies softly: 'And that's why we're all here now.'"

I look at Manú as I finish raising my coffee cup to my mouth. I must have stopped in mid-air while I was listening.

"Fantastic," I say. "What are you trying to tell me?"

"Our inner guru is made up of ancient wisdom and scientific knowledge. Are you with me?"

I have a light bulb moment, two to be exact. "No one is

walking ahead as our guide anymore. Instead an orientation, a sort of inner guide, is created within us."

Manú stares at me in surprise.

"Wow, where did that come from?"

"From the inner guru, of course," which earns me a thumbs up from Manú.

"My coffee is empty," I realise and say, "And my data storage seems to be full. I think we need to take a rain check. My system can't take any more coffee. Otherwise it'll collapse and the rest of me will fly out of the window in little pieces, and be dispersed all across the city."

"Let's not risk that. Let's break up camp and start the post-breakfast cleanup," says Manú and hands me the butter dish with a celebratory gesture. I take it, and without speaking, we return Manú's kitchen to its original harmonious, clean state.

Philosophy at the market

We're leaning on a tall table at an Italian coffee truck at Boxhagener Platz. They have the best latte macchiato in the market by far. It's the Saturday weekly market and for the aforementioned caffeine hit, we willingly interrupt our shopping for fresh fruit and vegetables.

I had spontaneously suggested the market for a chat. Surrounded by burning incense, beeswax candles, and tasty harvests from local farmers, it feels like the right location for today's discussion of energy.

"I've heard of chakras before. I have a friend who's into yoga and she talks about them as if it's so obvious. That always stopped me from asking more questions."

"Why?" Manú enquires.

"I didn't want to give the impression of wandering around like a nightshade in that regard."

"Most people in my yoga class care more about flexibility, health, and feeling good than spiritual depth. So there are more of your species in the garden."

When I finally get the joke, it's too late to respond or to laugh about it without her noticing. I laugh anyway.

In the meantime, Manú explains the basics of the chakras to me. She mentions something called nadis, which supposedly run through our bodies like little streams of energy.

"Two of the main nadi channels, Ida Nadi and Pingala Nadi, intertwine around our spine like two opposing waves. The seven crossings of the nadi streams make up the energetic centres: the chakras, and each has functions, characteristics, and links to certain organs. In the centre, in an almost straight line, the main channel Sushhumna Nadi rises to the crown chakra."

"Pardon me? Are we speaking the same language?"

Manú's inner professor stops her lecture.

"Can these energetic centres be measured?" I ask.

"Measured? No idea." Manú shrugs her shoulders. "You can measure body temperature, heart rate, and brain waves. So why not chakra energy?"

"Okay, so what kind of energy would that be?" I enquire, because something has just occurred to me.

"You ask tough questions." Manú ponders, but doesn't say anything.

"Apart from body temperature, it's all some kind of electricity, isn't it? Notice anything?"

"It's the same – inside and outside," Manú concludes, completely unimpressed. "Ayurveda and yoga take awareness further than body temperature and heart rate. You can imagine it as a sort of inner guidance. But it's basically like what we already talked about with the good and bad vibes..."

As if watching a movie, I see myself fall into water. I scramble to get back into the boat. The woman I adore is sitting in the canoe. She watches my failed attempts, laughing. Shame takes hold of me. I feel an incredibly strong pull below my navel.

"Hello, anyone home?" I hear someone call from far away. Manú looks at me expectantly and I feel like I've been caught not paying attention.

"Um, sure," I stammer, "I just remembered a situation when I felt an incredibly strong pull in my stomach. I wonder if that was chakra energy?"

"Sounds mysterious."

"Yeah, it was a canoe trip. Well, and I..."

"...don't want to talk about it," Manú finishes my stuttering sentence.

Sounds plausible, I think and although I'd have liked to say that, something stops me and I wonder who's taken the wheel now.

"If you put it like that, I wonder how awareness of the chakras works during yoga?" I try to deflect.

"And that's exactly why, by your request, you're coming to my place at 10 o'clock tomorrow morning, for your first yoga class." Manú grins from ear to ear and takes her time to take a big sip of coffee. I start feeling hot and have no clue which chakra is responsible.

"I know the feeling," Manú confirms.

"Know what feeling?" I reply astonished, because how can she read my mind yet again and see the thoughts dancing the polka in my brain?

"Being excited about doing yoga."

Does this look like excitement? – I refrain from saying that and manage a fake smile, which Manú accepts contentedly. She looks over at the Italian coffee truck's owner, who seems to already sense her wish for another latte macchiato.

"We are beings made of energy," she suddenly exclaims. This catches the attention of the couple at the next table and draws me back into our conversation.

"It sounds a little fantastical," I add matter-of-factly. "On the other hand: if it's proven that atoms are 99% empty and that there are electrical impulses and waves within our bodies, I can't really say that it's all crap."

We pause for a moment.

"Can you see energy?" Manú asks suddenly.

"See energy?"

"Yeah, it's possible to see a sort of energy field around plants and humans," Manú explains, as if it were the most normal thing in the world.

"And how does that work?"

"To start with, you take a blank background, like the sky. Then you softly gaze at a tree with the sky behind it. Try it!"

I slightly squint and relax. "I see something!" I burst out. The couple at the other table follow my gaze to the tree I'm looking at. They don't see anything and turn away.

"Aw, now it's gone."

"You have to keep not wanting it," Manú encourages me. "Try to let go of the excitement you experience when you gain awareness of something. As soon as you give in to the excitement, you won't see the veil of energy anymore."

"Fascinating." I keep practicing. The couple aren't quite sure whether someone's playing a joke on them.

"There it is again. And now it's gone again."

"Maybe this is a good time to end our spontaneous coffee meeting?"

I understand the deeper meaning of Manú's statement, as I follow her concerned look to the almost sold-out vegetable stand right across from us.

"Off I go to buy some 'Happy Cheese' then," I indirectly agree with Manú and we say goodbye, and head back into the hustle and bustle of the market.

For the sake of some energy

I'm standing in front of my wardrobe – clueless. What should I wear? This isn't something I usually ask myself. But in two hours and seventeen minutes, I'm supposed to turn up on Manú's doorstep for our meeting on the mat.

My thoughts wander back to gym class in sixth grade. There I am, slightly overweight and in shorts beside the high bar. Two people try to pull me up so I can swing my hips onto it. No chance – and I got a D for it. After my failed attempt at gymnastics, nobody wanted to touch the sweaty bar. 'Ew, that's gross!' I hear Kevin yell, as if he were still standing behind me right now. Everyone laughs, even the teacher, and I run out of the gym.

I put on the only pair of comfortable sweatpants I own. They're more suitable for jogging in the park in winter, but anyway. In the tram, I notice the slight trickling of sweat already, which only adds to my anxiousness.

"Come on in. We're all set."

Manú leads the way into the living room where two yoga mats are lying way too close to each other. I adjust them while Manú disappears into the kitchen for a moment. When she's back, she looks at me, smiles, and asks: "Ready?"

She's wearing a pair of black leggings and a tank top, with a short turquoise T-shirt over it. Her hair is braided. My T-shirt already feels a bit sweaty, which I try to ignore. We start and straight away I hear words like asana, sun salutation, prana, and bandha.

Far beyond my comfort zone, I try to figure out what I'm supposed to be doing here. I stretch myself into a deep lunge, pull up my arms with a jerk, and seem to have for-gotten to breathe altogether. I'm starting to see stars, but I can still hear Manú's calm, soft voice: "Let the breath flow, in and out. Relax your shoulders, enjoy the movement, wherever it takes you."

I slowly relax and let myself be guided. Where is this warmth coming from, this trust I have never felt before in such an uncomfortable situation? How does Manú manage to make it all feel so normal? No one's laughing while I, feeling stiff as a plank, struggle ungracefully. Is this real?

I sweat more than the situation requires and some sun-shaped splats start to appear on my mat.

"May I touch you?" asks Manú, standing very close to me now.

"Okay," I squeeze out and realize that I've forgotten to breathe again. Manú breathes in and out audibly. Then she gently pushes back my left shoulder. Her right hip is leaning on my back. As if by magic, my spine rotates a little bit further clockwise. Now I nearly manage to touch the floor with my left hand. She then corrects my right arm to point straight upwards.

"Slowly turn your head to look at your right hand. Breathe in, breathe out, in, out."

Her body is still lightly touching my back, as she slowly moves away, she says: "Trikonasana."

I try to hold the position by myself. Although I feel like a flag flapping in the wind, there's also a feeling of just being, lightness, or even calm. Is this surrender, the way it's described in meditation sometimes?

In a very uncomfortable shoulder stand position, I stretch my legs upwards as well as I can. The longer I stay in this position, the more the additional pounds around my stomach press onto my lungs. When Manú tries to help me reach my legs behind my head, I completely lose my breath.

"Whoopsie." Manú is startled when I regain my breath by rolling back up into a seated position. No wonder all yogis are lean machines, the fat ones all suffocated.

An hour later, I get to lie flat on my back to relax in Savasana. I've never felt as alive and relaxed as on this pink yoga mat in Erich-Weinert-Straße. I've already forgotten my shortness of breath from before. Yes, something is flowing through my body. If that's energy – wonderful! I can feel it like never before, and it's not a rush of blood – although there would be plenty of reasons for that.

I must have fallen asleep for a second. I suddenly hear Manú's voice.

"Stretch out and reach as far as you can. Turn to the side that lets you breathe more freely through your nose right now," Manú guides me softly, as if it's all perfectly natural.

Hmm, it's true, the left nostril seems a little stuffy and I turn to my right side before I get up.

"So, how was it? Too soft?"

I probably look at her as if I've just come back from another planet: "Wow, I'm..."

"...obviously speechless," Manú concludes correctly.

"I feel as if I'm being held by a magic hand, content, and full of energy."

"Ah, yes, energy. I left something out of the asanas. We'll get to that another time."

"What?"

"The conscious contraction of the stomach and pelvic

floor muscles. It's called closing the energetic locks – the bandhas."

"Bandhas?"

"Yes, you pull your navel towards your spine and then upwards. And you slightly contract your pelvic floor. It's almost like having to pee but still holding it in. Try it."

I'm completely overwhelmed by the exercise and the situation. How openly and entirely comfortably Manú talks about all of these things doesn't fit into the world view I've had up until now.

After a few failed attempts, she lets me off the hook with "It just takes some time" and I get a big glass of water from the kitchen.

"Do you want to shower here?"

"No, thanks, I'll do it at home. I have to leave anyway." After a short while, I'm standing on the street in my pants that now definitely feel way too warm and sweaty, and I don't really understand why I left so fast. The discomfort, the gym class memories, and, on the other hand, the support and warmheartedness during the last two hours have left me speechless and confused. What did Manú do to make me experience this sense of clarity? This feeling of being entirely okay and the relaxed way of being physically close during yoga is something I have to get used to. I have to laugh. We keep talking about energy and I think I know a thing or two about it. Crazy. Today I feel this energy inside of me and I don't know how to describe it.

After the shower, I feel very happy and secure in my own apartment. But I keep thinking about my first yoga session and the energising and light sensation that has stayed with me for the rest of the day. I'll probably have some very sore muscles tomorrow. Yep, this couch-potato could definitely use some more regular exercise. But first, I hit 'send'.

Thanks for this special, changing, and moving experience you call Ashtanga yoga.

Not changing...challenging

Energy – information – matter: when things become

The doorbell rings at Weichselstrasse 13. The small apartment on the fourth floor is where I call home. I like the cafés and the little park across the street with the big trees in the popular district of Friedrichshain. To me, it seems that the visitors to the park represent almost a complete cross-section of society. Although I'm more and more drawn towards places close to nature, I do enjoy the international vibe in the summertime in the German capital.

Meanwhile, it appears my guest has already made it up the stairs.

"Welcome, madame."

Manú responds to my greeting with a curtsey.

Then she goes into the kitchen to sit down. With her vintage-style, fringed dress, she looks like she's from the 1920s. Maybe she's some kind of time traveller and her friends are looking for her now, on September 28th, 1924 in Café Romantique at Breitscheidplatz between Budapester Straße and Kurfürstendamm. The twinkle in her eyes tells me that she has just come from one of those heated debates where women express their political opinion.

"And there's something else," she picks up the conversation as if she's addressing an audience, "Everything is energy. Everything vibrates. We're all connected that way. The universe guides our life. Whether we want it or not. Whether we know it or not. Whether we believe it or not."

"How can energy form a thought and then a cup? What do people do with the energy to produce a form?" I ask her.

"You tell me."

It's quiet. Where did all these people come from?

"Everything that exists began with a thought. Before the thought, that thought didn't exist," I begin hesitantly.

The listeners are silent.

"Energy can't just be created, but it can be transformed. It is given a form as a thought or an emotion. Information is produced."

"Bravo!" Manú cries, and everyone else seems excited too.

"Then something can manifest out of the information, a cup, for example." As I say this, I make a golden-blue cup appear from behind my hip. The crowd roars.

"Only now, more information can lead to using this cup, as a coffee cup, for example." Elegantly, I hand Manú the cup that's now filled with coffee. Applause from the crowd as Manú takes the first sip.

"Imagine," I continue, "energy is omnipresent. My consciousness arranges part of the energy in a way that produces information. The information will then be consolidated into forms that have a function."

"First it's a coffee cup and then I create the entire world!" Manú exclaims with excitement.

"If all thoughts and feelings are energy, my dear friends, which we can shape with our consciousness, then we can change the world. Then we are all God. Thank you for listening. Thanks so much. Thank you. Thank you."

I take a bow in front of the enthusiastic crowd. I suddenly hear a strange sound. A bell rings. Again and again. I search for the source in the crowd, which slowly dissolves into white fog. The ringing continues. I open my eyes. My twenty minute power nap is over. Where am I?

The doorbell rings at 13 Weichselstrasse.

"Everything alright?" Manú asks, as she notices the dazed look in my eyes.

I have no choice but to report the latest events to Manú in great detail. It takes a while before she calms down.

"That's really great!" Another episode of laughter follows before she asks, "So? And how do these extremely interesting and amusing discoveries about energy help us to answer our initial question?"

"Which was?"

"What's the difference between the energy that's outside and the energy that's inside me?"

"No idea. Maybe it's just another story."

CHAPTER 4

Faith, a Bridge to Knowledge

I believe I'm standing in a forest

The July heat had a firm grip on the city. So I decided to go spend some time in nature. I found refuge, a cabin and a real taste of the outdoors in the shady forest of Schorfheide. The washroom: a bowl under the cold water tap outside.

After a few days of hanging out on my own with the tall pine trees, an unmistakable rustle went through the bushes and a group of wild boars passed by the cabin grounds. The fence around the grounds that separated me from the animals does ease my mind a little.

Today, Manú wants to visit me because she likes the idea of pondering the questions of life in a natural setting. I pick her up from the train station.

Upon arrival at my hermitage, Manú looks around curiously. She stops when she sees the light blue portaloo: "Is that the only…"

"That's it, but it's very clean." The plastic door of the

toilet squeaks. She then moves on to inspect the open shed, which contains all sorts of knick-knacks.

"I would really love some coffee," she finally says. "Can your forest kitchen manage that?" Skeptically, she looks at the only source of water, a hose hanging from a tree. To her amazement, the first coffee is on the table in no time at all.

"So, do you believe in God?" I ask Manú.

"Thanks for the coffee." Then she ponders for quite some time.

"In India, I once heard someone say, 'I have to believe in God, as long as I haven't experienced him.' So, I'd have to say no."

I think about this briefly: "So you have experienced God?"

"I think so," Manú answers in the calm tone of voice I'm already familiar with from our yoga sessions.

"So believing would mean trusting something I don't know yet. Right?"

"Yeah, you could say that."

"In Christianity, faith seems to be more of an attitude that characterises you as an upright Christian," I add.

Manú looks at me in fake disbelief: "And what is an upright Christian in your opinion?"

"Someone who believes in Jesus, Mary, or God as an old man with a long beard, who all live together in heaven now. Also, an upright Christian goes to church, is baptised, confirmed, and married."

"But only once!" Manú adds.

I have to laugh and Manú shakes her head.

"So your upright Christian has to believe in these stories and act according to them. Is that right?"

"I think so," I respond, not quite sure. "What do you mean by saying that you've experienced God already? How so?"

Manú looks at me: "I think I need more coffee before I can answer that."

"Then let's let the forest kitchen surprise us again," I say and disappear into the cabin.

Only a short while later, I've managed to do exactly that. I present her with a coffee that will definitely surprise her.

"What's that?"

"Bulletproof coffee. It's great for oiling the cogs of cognition."

"What's that floating in it?"

"Coconut oil and ghee. Would you like some cardamom too?" I'm ready with the spice shaker.

"Don't you dare!" She quickly pulls the cup off the table and sniffs at it hesitantly.

"Go on, try it. I drink it almost every day. And now I'm extremely curious about your answer to the God question," I distract her. She takes the cue.

"To prove God means to doubt faith. That was the beginning of a philosophy class during my yoga teacher training."

"Wow. I mean..." I shrug my shoulders.

"Faith, to me, is a tool that helps me discover the unknown. Faith gives me an orientation and functions as a bridge to experiences."

"I like that idea," I respond, impressed. "And that's what you talked about in India?" Manú nods and skeptically takes a sip of the bulletproof coffee.

"Terrific."

"Maybe it's not as much of a big deal as we think. And definitely not all goody-two-shoes. Some devout believers wouldn't like these types of explanations at all."

"But it doesn't have a lot to do with Jesus on the cross and God in heaven," I note.

"More with science. Imagine, Einstein once had this idea about the warping of time. He believed in an idea and then proved it. To me, that's real faith."

"Although it's not understood that way in religion, I suppose."

"But it's kind of an inner strength, an emotion."

"So, according to your view, scientists are devout believers? I don't know how popular these ideas are, but you can count on my vote."

We sit in silence. I try to comprehend more clearly what Manú has just said. It feels like a riddle that somehow has the solution embedded in it. No clue.

"And how did you have that experience?"

Manú hesitates and searches for words. I sit there motionless, hanging on her every word.

"Can we take a rain check on that question?" In her eyes, I can see that she hopes I'll understand.

"Of course. Cheers!" I raise my cup. She smiles gently, but something seems to be on her mind.

"And you? What does faith mean to you?" she asks after a while.

"To me?" I repeat unnecessarily. "A story somebody tells. A fantasy story. Something like that. I don't really know."

Somehow Manú seems distracted, because she leaves what I just said uncommented. Then she takes her phone: "Do you have speakers here?"

"Yes."

"Go get them." She smiles mysteriously.

Then some music I've never heard before starts playing. "Do you remember the workshop, when Josua would sometimes put on music?" She begins to dance and encourages me to join her.

I somehow move as my heart starts to race and I laugh tensely. Then I jump into the air, to the left, then the right. What am I doing?

Manú dances effortlessly as if waves were moving through her body. Then the track ends and I rescue myself by heading towards my coffee mug.

She grins: "See, it changes the mood and pushes all your thoughts aside."

I nod in all directions and get two glasses of water.

"Wow, you really worked it," Manú says and points at my shirt, which is showing some new patterns.

"That always happens. No need to worry."

Manú dismisses it with a wave. "I'm not. It's just inner nature."

"I might as well just pour water on myself since it comes out right away again anyway."

Manú laughs. It honestly doesn't bother her?

Programming and the ego

"So tell me, does life get easier once I get closer to reaching my full potential?" she asks suddenly.

"If Josua is right, then yes," I respond.

"Then, what stops me? My inner programming?"

"Your programming?" I ask."It's Microsoft's fault?"

She chuckles and moves some hair out of her eyes. "No, I mean the habit of always reacting to certain situations in a specific way. Like not washing the dishes until the last cup and the last plate have been used."

"So, where do these programmes come from?" I dig deeper.

"Maybe they get installed while you're growing up? Or maybe, at some point, I reacted in a certain way and it worked. So I repeat the process until I do it without thinking about it."

I try to stay serious. Because the dancing has brought out my inner comedian, who now wants to make a joke out of everything. Right now, he's brainstorming about a not-having-to-wash-the-dishes-programme and how to use it. Being hungry or getting tired? Would they be enough to get out of it?

"If you find yourself in a similar situation later, the pro-gramme simply starts up," Manú finishes her thoughts.

"So at some point, we act quickly, following the same

patterns, without thinking about it, right?" I ask and look at Manú. "So we would just have to delete the programmes, as long as they're not write-protected, and all will be well," I combine the facts with playful, investigative skill.

I get a gentle slap on the wrist for the comment about write-protection.

"Are you messing with me?"

"Never!"

"Do you remember what Josua said about the ego?" she asks after sipping some water.

"No, I don't think so."

"On the second day, when the topic was anger, he talked about the death of the ego."

"Ah, yes. Do you remember Walter?" I ask in return.

Manú ponders for a moment: "Walter. Walter?"

"Heavy-built, in his mid-50s, with the overpowering aftershave."

"Oh, yes, that rings a bell."

"He was my partner during the anger exercise and he insulted me non-stop. Then we were supposed to dance out the anger."

"Yeah, exactly. I loved the idea and I still try it every once in a while. It really works," Manú enthuses. "How about you?"

"Well, I wouldn't go as far as saying I loved the idea, but it did work surprisingly well."

"That's exactly when Josua talked about letting go and the death of the ego. Then it would just be gone in some way."

"So let's say our ego is responsible for us always reverting to the same programmes, then it would have to be true for all our behaviour, not just the things we think are stupid, correct?"

I'm beginning to lose track. Death of the ego, using programmes, I feel like my whole life is on autopilot.

But Manú's on a roll now: "What happens when the ego is gone? What takes on all the jobs it was responsible for?" Manú looks at me expectantly.

"Can we postpone this one too, like your God experience?" I ask. "I need time to think."

Manú pauses. "Okay, I'll give you some time to think, even though I just got going." She closes her eyes and says to herself: "I'm letting go." She shakes her entire body and takes a deep breath in and out.

How generous, I think, and feel a little irritated by her comment.

Naturally in nature

"So, this means it's yoga time, right?"

I nod reluctantly. True, that was the plan. And suddenly two mats are laid out on the soft forest floor.

"You're pretty full of energy today."

Manú nods eagerly and prepares for the yoga session.

The flies sense opportunity and start circling above us in battle formation. I try hard to surrender to the harmony of the yogic movement. The trees sway gently in the wind as if to show me how to do it, but I still prefer to watch Manú.

At the end of the practice, I melt away. Just lying on my back and relaxing – Savasana is my favorite exercise already.

Suddenly I realise Manú will probably want to shower here.

"So, how's that going to work?" Manú asks with a glance at the only tap hiding behind two bushes. "Shower au naturale?"

I try to explain to her in detail my ingenious bathroom set-up and tell her I can just stay in the hut while she's doing it.

"Okay, so we heat the water, and then we use the tub there…"

I nod. "There's some shower gel too – organic, of course."

"Alright, here we go." By the time she reaches the washing station, she's already half undressed. I go inside the cabin, as promised, and wonder to myself: What am I doing here anyway?

Outside, I hear splashing and giggling. I see the water spraying over the bushes. Then I hear my name being called.

"Sorry, I think I left my towel in the kitchen."

Indeed. I find it by the fruit basket, together with her fresh clothes.

"Can you bring it to me, please? And my clothes must be somewhere there too."

I stretch my arm around the thick shrubbery and hand Manú her things. She laughs. "Sorry, and thank you.

Sometimes I just leave things all over the place. This is all fantastic!" A few drops of water land on my shirt.

What's much more distracting is how carefree she is being naked. Although I'm really trying not to look in her direction, I do notice a large tattoo that wraps around her left hip. I guess now's not the time to ask what it is and go back to the cabin.

A short while later, she's standing in front of me: "Your turn."

Carrying all my shower gear, I walk towards the water station. Manú has made herself comfortable with a book in front of the cabin and is enjoying the sun. I check the gaps between the bushes several times before I undress.

"Forget something?" Manú asks when I come back after the shower.

"All done."

"Really? Do you practice silent, high-speed showering? I thought you hadn't even started yet."

"It's wonderful here in the forest and I love these trees," I reply quickly.

Then I discreetly slip my things into a bag and hang my towel up on the line.

Completely relaxed, I lean back on the bench in front of the cabin.

"Aren't you getting hot?" Manú asks.

I look down conspicuously at my long-sleeved shirt, sweatpants, and running shoes. "I'm fine."

Manú is sitting in shorts and a tank top in her usual lotus position and turns another page of her book. My eyes are glued to a bird jumping from branch to branch in the tree. How interesting.

Later, the usual suspects, bread, cheese, coffee, and a still wrapped piece of cake, are ready on the table.

"Bohème naturale," Manú calls this midweek meeting and smiles at me with satisfaction. Then she cuts open a roll. The top half waits to be garnished with butter, cheese, and some lettuce.

CHAPTER 5

From the Ego to the Unknown

Ego – the grass is always greener

The sun is high in the blue sky, little specks of colour decorate the bright green of the grass. The blue, orange, and yellow flowers of the various herbs that grow on the Drachenberg in Grunewald make it look especially pretty. In front of us, the vista of the city unfolds. Up here, far away from the hustle and bustle of the city's streets, Berlin appears peaceful, soft, almost lovely.

The perfect atmosphere for today's breakfast location – picnic style. On the blanket, two cushions, a thermos, two mugs, and some other requisite accessories for a sophisticated culinary treat. Everything seems perfect, but Manú is looking out at the scene with an unusually pensive look on her face.

I pour some coffee: "How are you doing?"
"Alright."
I take a sip of almond-milk coffee and try to find my orientation in the cityscape in front of us.

"Has someone rearranged the buildings?" I ask. "A change of perspective – literally."

Manú sips her coffee and I decorate the meadow breakfast spread with some flowers and stalks of grass. She smiles timidly.

"Imagine me being a bit quiet and withdrawn, how would you try to cheer me up?"

Tensely I wait for what seems like an eternity for her to answer, which sends my temperature soaring. Or no, that's probably the sun.

"Oh, you know," Manú starts, "I met up with a friend of mine yesterday. She told me about how she's training to become a life coach." She puts a little too much emphasis on the words 'life coach'.

"Mmm. And what's wrong with that?" I enquire.

"She's even started offering counseling sessions. Her first workshop is coming up soon and she already has eight people signed up."

"A quick question." Manú looks up. "Why are you showing me five fingers when there are eight people in the workshop?"

She laughs and softly gives my shoulder a shove. "Shut up."

She plays with the flowers on the blanket. "I think it's great, really. But somehow, I don't know. Something isn't right. Something's not right with me, I think."

"What might be wrong?"

She looks straight at me and, a little louder, she says: "I should be happy for her, right?"

I nod. "Am I correct in assuming there's a 'but' coming?"

"It made me sad, even angry to watch this fireworks display of information and excitement. When I got home, I was exhausted. I felt so small and completely incapable."

"Oh." I didn't see that coming. "Why?"

"I asked myself the same question."

"Did you find an answer?" I ask encouragingly.

"Well, I just started writing some things down."

She stops talking and I would love to say something more encouraging. But what? There's nothing I'd like better than if everything were just okay now. What can I do? How can I help her? I look over in her direction. She's digging in her pockets.

"Can I read something to you?" she asks hesitantly.

"Of course."

She finds a piece of paper in her other pocket. She unfolds it.

"So, I just wrote some stuff and I have no idea if it makes any sense."

"No problem. I'll ask if something is unclear."

She takes a deep breath: "Okay." She looks at me and then turns the paper the right way round to start reading.

"Why am I doing this? Why do I look at the shadows and then feel small and useless? My head is spinning. Fuck this. And Hanna? She lives a happy life while I'm always struggling with all this inner work. The shadow self! Maybe it doesn't exist and I'm just chasing a phantom? She's successful and keeps growing because she's not afraid to start something new. – Hanna, by the way, is the friend I talked about."

"I thought so."

Manú searches for the sentence where she left off. "Maybe every once in a while, she doesn't have a good day either. But then she saves herself with these spiritual 'offerings' and everyone loves it. The 'amazing' feedback balances out her bad days. That's where she gets her energy from and she's happy most of the time. Of course, she shows that to me, and I can't even manage not to judge her. I hate myself for thinking this way, and I'm scared that I'll never manage to do anything. It feels like complete shit."

Manú looks at me.

"Wow. I wouldn't be brave enough to just read something like that out loud."

"I just don't want to give this story – and it's really not more than that, right? – so much power. And when I write it down and read it to you, then... I don't know, it feels a bit lighter and easier afterwards."

I'm impressed and nod my head.

"There's a bit more."

"Sorry, I didn't mean to interrupt you."

"The fact that she's understanding, shows sympathy, and gives me advice makes me even angrier. At the same time, she sincerely believes that she acts kindheartedly and lovingly towards me – the poor little thing. I feel like a helium balloon someone let the air out of and I just sink to the ground. Why am I on this spiritual path? Why am I searching for the truth, why do I want to wake up? Other people just do their thing without having to dig so deep.

And then they offer seminars and tell the world how it's supposed to spin.

"I'm angry! But at what?

"At Hanna? At myself?

"Why?

"Why am I not teaching seminars? Why don't I do it?

"Am I too afraid? Is that why I'm angry at Hanna because I'm too scared? And because she just does it, although she doesn't know everything yet?

"Shit. Why does everyone else just do things? In such a fun, showy and glamourous way too! They're successful and I'm just pissed off."

Manú stops for a second:

"I'm angry about the fact that I judge people for what they do, instead of just letting them be and focusing on making my own contribution to the world."

Only now, I notice that she's stopped reading from her piece of paper. "Where did that come from?"

"What?"

"Well, what you said just now."

"I don't know."

"Thanks for your openness. That was ready for the press."

Slightly embarrassed, she looks at the ground. I rescue myself with a sip of coffee, gripping my mug tightly.

What I really want to say to her is this: I know these doubts. And I think it's great how clearly you can see that it's about acceptance – about wanting to feel. Maybe that's all that's needed. I bet most people are familiar with the need to compare and compete. But I also bet most people are not ready to admit it, write it down, and read it out loud the way you just did. Your emotions towards your friend may be absolutely valid. It's so easy to get addicted to the drug of approval.

That's what runs through my brain. I would love to tell her, but I can't get the words out for some reason. Manú looks at me. She seems relieved and there's a sparkle in her eyes again. So I suggest: "Come on, let's celebrate your courage!" Manú nods her head in agreement and I pour some more coffee, hand her a roll and make myself a sandwich with cheese, lettuce, and some bright orange edible flowers. Half of it lands on the picnic blanket as soon as I take the first bite.

Hello, here I am

Manú has given our meetings a bold title: "Breakfast with Buddha and Jesus." Only she could come up with something like that and although I'm not very serious about religious correctness either, my inner officer of ethics and morals is ringing the alarm bells. I tend towards agreeing with him.

"I have deeper conversations with you than with anyone else I know."

This compliment interrupts my inner debate on the

name for our meetings. "I like the title you gave them. Funny idea."

"I think so too," Manú confirms.

"So, who are you in this duo?" I ask, considering the biological facts.

"The divine doesn't have a gender."

How does she always manage to slip out of near-impossible situations?

I change the topic. "I would really love to move my body a bit again soon."

Manú furrows her brow and asks, "What else – other than yoga – could move the body in a leisurely, healthy, and fun way?"

A victorious grin creeps across my face. "Squash."

"Squash?"

"Yes, that fulfills all your requirements – leisure, health, and fun."

"And where does one play squash?"

I think for a second. "On a squash court."

Manú doesn't even blink despite my response, which I thought was rather witty.

"Okay, then let's go play squash."

Three days later, Manú is holding a squash racket in her hands for the first time. "This is so much fun!"

I duck out of the way to avoid a ball. "It totally clears your head," I say.

An hour later, we're standing in front of the sports centre – satisfied and relaxed.

"Do you want to grab a drink?" I suggest hesitantly.

Once we've arrived at the bar, Manú orders non-alcoholic beers, which arrive at our table just moments later.

"No alcohol?" I notice.

"It's for the better," she says. "I don't want you dancing on the tables later."

Although the chance of that happening is minimal, minuscule, to be exact, I accept.

"Well then, cheers."

"Cheers."

"Manú, I did something."

She stops drinking her beer. "What?"

"Your story from the other day. I just couldn't let it go. I somehow got the feeling that it also was about what we refer to as the ego. I did some research and let my fantasy run wild a little bit."

"You let your fantasy run wild? You're really good at building up excitement anyway. Did you know that?"

"No. But coming from you, I'll take it as a compliment. Thanks…"

"You're welcome. But now it's about time to let the cat out of the bag."

"Okay. It's a story about how the ego starts its job."

Manú looks at me as if I've said that I'm from a planet called Forty-Two. "Will I just read it to you?"

"Most definitely!"

I pull a folder with a single sheet of paper out of my backpack. Manú looks at me attentively while she takes two sips of beer.

"A body connects with a soul – it gets born into it. But something's missing."

"Wait a second. Born into a soul? I've never heard of that," Manú realises.

"Well, I heard it in a video, a talk with a Buddhist monk. If the soul is eternal, then the body, which is something transitory, has to be born into it."

"Hmm...right. And in the end, the soul leaves the body," concludes Manú. "Okay then, go on. Sorry for interrupting."

"In that moment, a piece of energy separates itself from universal existence and starts moving. The energy approaches the little human body at great speed and disappears inside it.

"'Hello?' No answer. 'Cuckoo. Here I am.'

"This wasn't language, but something definitely seems as if it has just spoken. The ego looks around. Nothing. Or maybe...? The ego discovers a large machine with lots of buttons and little screens. It checks its small notebook and realises: 'This must be the mind. But how does it work?'"

Manú suddenly laughs. "Sorry."

I cough slightly and straighten my back. I take another sip of beer and wish it were a real one.

"The ego flips through the pages of its notebook. There are different chapters:

"*In Darkness and Light* – there's very little information in that part and what's there is cryptic and hard to understand. 'Death is the end of everything.' What is that? Death? It also says: 'The light reveals itself with the one.' What does that mean? And then: 'Love is everything.' This seems to be important. Love and emotional security come from mum and dad, it continues. If that's where love and a sense of security come from, those two humans will receive the most attention."

"Question." Manú raises her arm and giggles.

I look up and she asks: "So how does this ego suddenly know that love is so important and comes from your mum and dad?"

I look confused and check my piece of paper. "The notebook explains it," I respond with relief.

"Okay, and how did your ego get the notebook?" Manú asks slowly for emphasis.

"I read somewhere that humans can inherit experiences. Crazy, right?"

"I see, and someone wrote all this into a notebook, which now belongs to your ego," Manú concludes.

"It's not meant literally," I add, so I don't immediately get attacked again.

"I volunteer as a fact-checker before you send that story to the New York Times." She laughs again. Was it really that funny?

"I'll continue," I say, slightly annoyed, because I don't know what's going on with Manú. She takes another sip of her non-alcoholic beer.

"A bit confused, the ego keeps flipping the pages of the n-o-t-e-b-o-o-k," I emphasise every single letter. "*Pre-birth.* It reads, followed by a few scribbles: 'Loud voices, fast running – be careful!' Or: 'Love – no. The pain isn't worth it.' And: 'Your troubles will be the beginning of your salvation.'

"What's that supposed to mean? How's that supposed to help?"

Manú bursts out laughing again. The difference this time is that she can't stop. "Sorry, Tom. But it sounds a little bit like an IKEA construction manual. I'm not surprised that humans are so messed up if we're supposed to function according to a manual like that."

I feel pretty stupid. "What's that supposed to mean?" I ask grumpily.

"I'll be right back." She laughs and gets up, holds on to the table, and then heads towards the toilet.

Is she drunk? From the non-alcoholic beer? I look at the bottle. Why did she...? She's back at the table already.

"Uhm, I think I'm going to head home. Something feels weird."

"Well, you just downed an entire beer in no time."

"I did what?" she enquires, as if she has no idea what I'm talking about.

I bring her to the door. "Should I walk you home?"

"No, I'm alright, Mr Author." She waves to me, as she walks down the stairs to the subway station extra carefully.

Lost and confused, I'm left standing on the street, alone. What was that about?

I go home, but I can't let go of what just happened. In the kitchen, my eye catches two bread rolls. I add cheese, mayo, mustard, and ketchup. Some greens and my DIY-burgers are done. My thoughts disappear into the plot of a Netflix movie. Soon I'm holding a second burger in my hand. I also find a beer in my fridge; the half-empty bottle is now next to my laptop and a bag of chips. I didn't mean to finish the pudding, but the pot is empty now. I find an open packet of salted peanuts in my junk food cabinet. The movie couldn't be any more cheesy. In the end, they end up together and everyone is happy, except for me. Without any motivation or energy left, I drag myself for a brief visit to the bathroom and then to bed. I feel terrible.

It's a restless night. When I wake up, it's almost nine. My stomach is bloated and I feel like a fully loaded rubbish truck. Why did Manú make fun of my story? I'm such an idiot for reading something half-finished to her. Did I offend her? But how?

I guess that's the end of our meetings then. I messed it up again. Typical. "Damn it!" I yell from the shower as what's leftover from my late-night dinner suddenly wants to come out. Maybe I can explain to her again what I meant with the whole ego thing?... I put my phone down. Playing squash really was such fun, but why the food binge then? I hate myself for it. I should go for a run today. The heartburn reminds me that I meant to add healing clay to my tea. Gross. I close the door behind me and drag myself through the park. I feel a sting in my right side and soon I'm out of breath. Come on! Keep going! My next toilet visit is becoming more urgent. If Manú saw me like this, she probably wouldn't want anything to do with me anyway. Who would want to be with someone like this?

Old English style?

The next morning, a repeated 'bing' wakes me up.

> Hey!

> Do you have time to meet today?

> I could be at CaffeinCentral this afternoon. How about 4? 😜

> That works. See you then. Thanks 🙏

Does she want to apologise? Or is this goodbye? I definitely want to ask her why she disappeared so quickly. Or is it about the alcohol?

Does she drink regularly? Maybe she has a drinking problem. If only I hadn't read that stupid story to her. After she trusted me with her deepest thoughts and feelings during our picnic, I go and ruin it all with some silly anecdote. Half past three. I need to go, but even getting up feels like a hurdle. Should I cancel?

All the outdoor tables at the little CaffeinCentral in Mainzer Straße are taken, so I go inside to order some coffee. At ten past four, I count the fifth time I look at the vintage clock on the wall. And then suddenly she's coming towards me with swift steps and breathes out a believable "Sorry! Have you been waiting for long?"

"No, no. I just got here."

She takes off her bike helmet and looks at the menu. When she sits down at the table with a latte macchiato, I distinctly notice my heartbeat.

Manú takes a deep breath: "Oh God, it was awful. I'm so sorry for the stupid way I treated your story..." She looks at me with a sorry look on her face.

"Didn't you notice something wasn't right with the beer?" I ask.

"No. Well, much too late. I was so thirsty from our squash session that I just finished half the bottle in no time. And we were so caught up in our conversation. Once I noticed what was going on, I just wanted to leave. I was so embarrassed!"

"I didn't check the label either," I respond, with a noticeable sense of relief. Then I have to laugh. "You definitely had me quite confused."

"You're telling me! I had a headache from it yesterday. I normally don't drink alcohol. I'll pay better attention next time, I promise."

"Okay. For what it's worth, you have a good story to tell your grandkids one day now," I say.

"So, what happens to the ego next?" Manú enquires.

"I'm sorry I read the first draft to you without having it proofread. I usually don't do that. You shared so much about yourself, and then I come along..."

"What are you talking about?" asks Manú. "I thought it was so brave of you just to read that obviously rough version of the story."

"Really?" I feel a tingle of excitement.

"Yes, what did you think? I love the idea of the ego taking on a job somehow."

"In the story, I imagined a rather simple life during childhood. That's why I chose language that kids would understand."

"Knowing that helps. Your ego seemed a little bit intellectually challenged to me." Carefully, Manú tries to explain why, under the influence, she thought it was so funny a couple of days ago.

"One time when I was a child, I ran out into the street," Manú continues. "A car just barely missed me and my mum made a huge scene afterwards. I still remember that. The idea that something like that is stored in some kind of archive is pretty funny."

"And I remember the drama I made when it came to doing my homework," I say. "It was a constant battle with my mum that always came with 'You're not going outside until...'"

"I'm pretty sure we're not made for this kind of school system," Manú asserts.

"What do you mean?"

"Well, if I look at it from your story's perspective, then the ego must be pretty confused when at six or seven years old it suddenly has all these things it has to do, seemingly out of nowhere. It was okay to react to the present moment, then suddenly it's all about the future. Suddenly the ego is supposed to sit still, be quiet, and listen at school for hours on end."

"If our parents had had a traumatic school experience like that, the notebook would probably mention them," I reflect.

"Why don't you ask?"

"Who should I ask?"

"Your ego."

"That's some idea," I respond.

Manú recollects: "When I felt like I truly understood something in school, I was always so excited. My elementary school teacher didn't get it all." She shakes her head.

After a short silence, she decisively announces: "I believe that if this ego truly exists, its purpose is to immediately react to certain situations."

"You don't have to convince me," I respond.

"Do you want to go to the flea market on Sunday?" Manú asks.

"Are we going to visit your ego, or is there another reason?"

"My bathroom needs some attention. I'm looking for a new lamp and some cool decor. Decoration and design are my passion. I love when things look a little quirky, but are functional."

"How about a knitted cover for your toilet seat?" I suggest.

"I see we're on the same page. I really want to give my bathroom an unusual and cool vibe. Have any ideas?"

"Yes," I say, after I've brought us two more coffees.

Manú looks at me with wide eyes. "I'm all ears."

"What do you do in your bathroom?"

"How much detail do you need?"

"Using the toilet and physical hygiene would be sufficient answers, for example," I say to avoid the worst.

"Okay," Manú keeps pondering, "I hang my clothes to dry there, store towels and cosmetics, and the cleaning supplies need somewhere too."

"Anything else?"

"Well," Manú blinks a few times. "I like to read in the bathtub, so some books might come in handy."

I think aloud: "Bookshelf, reading during a relaxing bath, with candlelight and maybe some relaxing music?"

"Sounds good."

"What do you think about old English style?" I ask.

"How do you mean?"

"Well, like in an old English living room, in green, red, and gold. Then something wooden; and a touch of kitsch."

"The Mauerpark flea market is the perfect place for that." Then Manú ponders, "Maybe we'll find two porcelain dogs or some fake pink flowers. And..."

"...an old leather armchair ?" I add.

"Maybe."

"When it comes to knitted covers, I suggest adorning the rolls of toilet paper instead of the toilet seat," Manú unexpectedly rejoinders my ironic comment and allocates me the knitting job. "Perfect plan! Let's meet Sunday at two at Mauerpark. Coffee's on me."

At the market – deeds are done

At the market, we gradually merge with the streams of people moving between the stands and then stop next to a box, out of which a light brown lampshade is peeking. The pattern has little red roses and dogs with pink bows. We get it for 15 Euros. The seller forces a smile. Maybe he can't shake the feeling that he went too low with the price for this extraordinary piece of art. Manú is a hardcore haggler.

We stop at another stand with all kinds of unnecessary knick-knacks.

"I was thinking," says Manú, "could it be that the ego learns more through spiritual work?"

I think about it, but can't quite imagine what she means. "Do you have an example?"

"yoga could be a good one. When I manage complicated poses like headstand or lotus and know what Trikonasana and Savasana mean, it's easy to feel special."

"You mean the ego develops to its own benefit because it uses the new skills?"

Manú picks a ceramic figure off of a table. It's a cat, a pretty awful one, which forces me into distracting her from it.

"I have an example too," I interject.

"Let's hear it."

"Are you familiar with the concept of closed-ended questioning?"

"Not really, no. What is it?"

"You're talking to someone who's completely outraged.

By repeating the person's last sentence or thought, you make them say 'yes', which moves you onto common ground and away from the rage."

"How do you know this?"

"I learned it at a communication seminar. Conflict management."

"And what's so egocentric about it?" Manú asks.

"You can use the technique of asking closed-ended questions to manipulate someone by creating these 'yes'-confirmations again and again."

"Wow. I have to be careful from now on then."

"I wouldn't worry. Considering your quick mind, I'd be walking on thin ice."

"...walking on thin ice?"

"Yes, exactly."

To my relief, in the meantime, Manú has left behind the cat.

"Sometimes, I hear about having to let go of one's ego, giving it up or even letting it die," Manú says.

"True, we've talked about that before," I recall.

"So I wonder who, if not my ego, is supposed to react when someone calls my name. Is there something like an beyond-ego?"

"Not sure I can offer a satisfying answer."

"Observing my thoughts helps me," Manú says and slowly moves on to the next table. "I often ask myself who's talking and whether I should believe the speaker."

"There's someone talking?" I ask in disbelief. "You mean some kind of voice that gives advice every once in a while?"

"Yeah, exactly like that."

I have to think. "Isn't it kind of difficult to constantly be in observation mode?"

"You can practice," Manú replies.

"Especially when things get a little heated, I can't imagine it being very easy."

"It's not a complete disaster if you fail to be observant for a few minutes now and again."

Did she really just say that?

"It's all just a matter of practice, and it takes time for it to work more than a couple of minutes. You're basically never done practicing, your whole life. I also drop out of it sometimes when random things trigger me."

Because of the comment from earlier, I'm having a hard time focusing.

"Like these two adorable dogs, for example." Manú picks up two brown, teacup-sized hunting dogs with long ears. They do look pretty cool, but I'm afraid the hopeful-looking saleswoman will probably not make her sale of the day.

"The fact that I'm carrying the dogs now – is that part of my consultation work for your bathroom?" I ask, after they try for the second time to bite my back through the backpack.

"You're asking whether carrying the accessories for my bathroom is part..."

"Yes, yes. It has to seem natural when you're using the closed-ended question technique."

Manú giggles.

"It doesn't work if the other person knows the method

or if you think about it for too long. Right now, both cases apply.”

“Okay, I get it and would like to express my gratitude, also in my ego’s name, for the helpful explanation.”

And so we move on and collect all kinds of things that will create the old English style in Manú’s bathroom. Eventually, we get two cups of coffee and sit down on a park bench to people-watch.

“Does the ego manage to do everything by itself?” Manú asks after a long pause.

“What do you mean?”

“When I look inside myself, I see very different modes of behavior. Rejection, wishes, fears, and so on. If the ego manages all this by itself, it must be pretty talented, right?”

“Hmm...no idea. Sounds like a very stressful job,” I comment.

“It would be so great if you could visit it, this multi-talented ego.” Manú looks at me expectantly.

My ego doesn’t seem to care, because it’s still angry that we missed the chance of getting a piece of cheesecake from the bakery stand. But I just had to win this one. Otherwise, I would have discredited myself entirely in front of Manú. The other day I proudly announced that I had turned my back on cheesecake. She was skeptical, as she already knows about my fondness for cake.

“This marriage will last. Come whatever,” was her opinion. This had given me the added incentive to finally take a stronger stand against this weakness. No, definitely not, I haven’t eaten cake for weeks, I confirmed to myself.

"Would you come with me if we knew where to go to visit the ego?" Manú asks and tears me out of my cheese-cake daydream.

I nod, and I'm almost sure she thinks it's possible.

"Visit the ego; now that's some idea!"

Birthday and Spirits I Summoned

The spirits I summoned

I'm sitting on my pillow, legs crossed, my left foot in front of my right. I can't get anywhere near the effortlessness with which Manú puts herself into the lotus position. I have to smile. My body doesn't seem designed for such things, which is okay, most of the time. Still, I add that thought to all the others on a little cloud and let them pass by with the next deep breath.

I start to feel calmer, adjust my upright sitting position one more time, relax my face muscles along with my stomach, and feel how an invisible force lets go of my shoulders so that they slowly begin to sink lower. Am I really ready for this?

"A guardian, what is that anyway? Following a dream. This has to stay between us," the inner commentator's voice whispers into my right ear – from the inside.

"I'm going to put you on a cloud with the others if you don't stop with that nonsense," I say sharply to the voice inside myself.

"Okay, okay."

Now there's silence and I recognise the tree, which has an opening in it where some steps lead down towards the river. Just like before, I get into the canoe and paddle out into the main current. I pull up on the narrow sandbank on the opposite side of the river, get out, and walk up to the flower-scented meadow. And now?

This kind of visualisation has led me to the other world before. Out of curiosity and just because, I once let Eric guide me through this shamanic journey. Later, I was more than surprised by the clarity of what happened in it and the answers that were revealed to my questions. So now I'm trying to get in touch with this other world again.

While I'm heaving all of these thoughts onto a massive cloud so they can drift away out of my head, something moves in the thick forest directly across from me. A short time later, a soft, low voice speaks: *"Be here and listen, following the question. Answers will be revealed, disguised in the splendour of words."*

Visualising myself bowing to this being, I ask for support in the quest to find what I want to reveal itself as ego, as this one ego. We walk over to the other end of the meadow, where there's a view stretching far into the distance. White, shimmering cloud cover below us obscures the view to the bottom of the vast plain.

"A universe in the human, a not-place in existence. A life developing, so eternally limited."

I carefully listen to the words of this being, who's wearing a pheasant feather on the right side of his beret. Inappropriately for the situation, his warm-hearted presence gives me a sense of security. I look down at the clouds with a joyful sadness and a sense of vitality. This is what home feels like, I think, but there's nothing here, or is there? Then I hear the deep voice warmly say: *"When ready for knowledge, no place for wanting. To be open in this love, you feel it, will you follow it?"*

"I am ready, I hear you. Please, do you have answers for me?" A little uncertain, yet determined, these words form in my mind.

He nods to me and says: *"Ready for the energy in the many, which appears in the physical face. Do you see how left and right drive you into the always wanting? The having here as mine, not yours is all action's basis. Do you want to be able to accept it, when no escape can follow?"*

Before I can reply, he disappears as suddenly as he had appeared. I keep walking. In a small, wooded area, I suddenly find myself in front of a dilapidated cabin. At its entrance, on a moss-covered table, lies a richly decorated scroll of paper – the table of gifts. I remember my last shamanic journey, where a squirrel brought me a nut. No squirrel in sight, but a cheerful sparrow flies around me, chirping. *"Remember and accompany, when he will follow the full moon's path,"* the wise man had also just said. Was he talking to the sparrow or me?

As it lands on the table, I slowly move closer. I hesitate at first, but then I carefully unroll the thick paper. *If you call strange lands your teacher, then the journey is your home. Farewell, oh ordinary life, a refuge of comfort and dungeon of emotions.* Is that my future? I have to swallow and it seems to have gotten hot.

I take a deep breath in and out, my hand already on the handle of the rotten door. Is this the cabin of the lost parts of souls, as it's called in shamanic journeys? If so, this would be the last part of the journey. Slowly, the door opens, as if by an invisible hand. Pure joy rushes towards me. The luminous yellow light provides a stark contrast to the weather-beaten cabin. Overwhelmed, I enter and a patch of light slowly moves towards me, then disappears into my chest. I breathe quickly. Tears fill my eyes. It feels as if a desire has been fulfilled, a reunion after far too long.

Outside, the sparrow is chirping, full of excitement and joy as I make my way back to the river, get into the canoe, and paddle back. The sparrow balances skillfully on the edge of the canoe, despite its rocking. Then I climb up the steps and feel – my body, my breath, the cushion, the space around me. I'm back. I stretch and, a bit embarrassed, wipe the tears from my face. How did this happen? Then, slightly startled, I see: by my open window, some greyish brown sparrows land in the tree, chirping excitedly in my direction. I raise my eyebrows, rub my face and neck. I'm sweating slightly and can feel my heart beating. Whatever I just thought, dreamed, experienced – the fact that I remember every detail can't be ignored.

I write down the wise man's words and the ones from the paper scroll. I carefully fold the piece of paper and write "Sparrow, 21 days" on the outside and put it on my living room shelf. I remember Eric saying that it would take 21 days to absorb and integrate the experiences of a shamanic journey. In the beginning, I pick up the note daily, visualise the sparrow and try to understand the wise man's words. But gradually, day to day life and some other confusing meditations make the memory of what I experienced start to get more and more blurry.

One night

I toss back onto my left side for the seventh time this hour. Wide awake is an apt description for the state I'm in at 0:48 in my bed. If I said I don't know why I can't sleep, I'd be lying. There aren't any more clouds where I can put the thought that my brain is continuously reproducing. My body freezes in a state of shock if I even think about telling Manú what I experienced in the past week. I know I won't get away with my famous mysterious half-statements this time. Not when it comes to this topic.

Taking five shamanic journeys in three weeks isn't exactly clever. Of course, there are some repercussions. But should all our conversations, all the breakfasts, remain nothing but a little bit of diversion, some entertainment in the never-ending analysis of things? Nothing is clearer than the knowledge that these conversations will slowly dissipate if we don't dare to go deeper. And it looks like I'm going to have to expose myself, open up about my feelings. It's never been as clear as it is now, after this last journey.

Manú did it. She made herself vulnerable, up there on the Drachenberg when we had our picnic. She showed empathy when I was doing yoga for the very first time. She just shows her feelings so easily, while I was just rattling at some of my jammed doors, trying to open them, to no avail. Now I'm actually at a point where I can just unscrew all the door hinges and open up, with all my doubts and fears. To experience who I am – who I also am. Unfortunately, this requires me telling Manú the whole story and asking her whether she…

Even my thoughts freeze when I try to finish the sentence in my head. Again, I throw myself onto my other side, as if I'm trying to tear myself free from something. Snuggles, my little white-grey stuffed dog with the floppy ears, is catapulted out of the bed. Maybe the time for him to move out is approaching, it's way overdue. I wonder if he knows it's coming?

I wake up exhausted and it takes a few minutes before I can decipher the numbers on my clock: 8:23. I peel myself out of bed. It feels as though I just finished a marathon three hours later than the target time. The tap in the shower is set to ice-cold for some reason and my tired system receives a wake-up call it can't ignore. I shower for longer than necessary at a comfortable temperature and step onto my shower mat, feeling squeaky clean. "yoga is always now" it reads in large letters.

I look at it in disbelief. It looks back. How did this all-knowing accessory make it into my bathroom? The last person I let into my apartment yesterday for a short visit was Manú.

> Good morning!
> Listen, do you know anything about shower mats that have words of wisdom printed on them? My inner slug feels provoked.

Half an hour later, my phone lights up with an answer.

> Happy Birthday!
> Let your feelings dance.
> I'm excited about meeting your friends tonight.

'Panic!' my mind announces and immediately sends all the thoughts from last night onto the stage dancing a conga line. Emotions waltz in almost immediately. It's too late to tell my friends about Manú now. It looks like everything's going to happen at the same time tonight. I look at myself in the mirror: Happy birthday, old friend. We can do this!

An almost harmless birthday party

In the evening, my guests slowly arrive. A short while after, there's a pink teddy bear sitting next to a fake wedding proposal, a little box I won't open until tomorrow to be on the safe side, red roses, a bottle of banana liquor, and a cheesy happy birthday banner. Who needs enemies with friends like these? But I love them all.

Manú isn't here yet and I've missed the opportunity to announce her somehow. I know my friends know how to behave, but there are reasons not to be 100% sure. The bell rings in the middle of a lively conversation. The room falls silent and someone asks: "Is anyone else coming?" The alarm bells go off inside me, and with a shaky "Yes" I rush to the door.

"Happy birthday again!" Manú hugs me and whispers, "I'm happy we met," into my ear.

I smile sheepishly and nod my head in agreement with her.

"Isn't anyone else here yet?" she asks, surprised.

"In the living room," I answer.

My momentarily silent guests sit there in suspense. All of them bolt upright and staring at the door. My brother Rick is standing by the window holding on to his beer glass. I've regained my composure and my inner comedian ceremoniously proclaims, "Welcome to gopher country."

Manú laughs and apologises immediately, but the scene really is very funny. I introduce Manú to the gophers and my brother is sharp enough to start asking some questions so that the atmosphere slowly starts to relax.

But it's not long till I'm sweating again. Manú is looking curiously at the gift table, when Paul comes back from the bathroom and another secret is revealed: "So what's up with your shower mat?"

"It's a gift from Manú," I inform him.

"Well then, Manú's gift must be presented on the gift table." Paul has already left and comes back with the 'yoga is always now' shower mat.

Silence. Manú has a hard time assessing the situation and looks around questioningly. "Dude, are you doing yoga now?!" Rick finally asks.

"Yeah, why not?"

"Well, because you always had a lot to say against it," Paul explains and puts the corpus delicti with the other gifts. His amazement is not feigned.

"Times change and so do people," I reply calmly. But my friends wouldn't be my friends if they were satisfied with that explanation.

"Why the sudden change of heart? I mean, if anyone in this group has been arguing against yoga for decades, it's our birthday boy."

I'm running out of arguments and I feel a slight temperature rise under my shirt. With the next few sentences and the tortured laughter that follows, I've practically handed myself to them on a plate.

"Alright, I admit it. Through Manú here, I have started to enjoy yoga. She explained it to me in such a cool way."

Heatwaves accompany these few words and my throat is dry.

Everyone seems busy trying to sort this new information somehow. I didn't know that I had been so convincing with my anti-yoga arguments in the past few years.

"So you just decided to start one day?" Rick asks again.

"Yeah, I just gave it a try."

"But rumor has it, it wasn't an easy road." With these words, Manú loosens up the situation again and adds a wink for good measure. The chatter slowly starts up again, but the main topic remains: How long have you been doing this? What was the first time like? As we talk, I find out that the vast majority of my friends are open-minded about yoga. This comes as a surprise to me – apparently only to me.

The evening ends satisfactorily. After all the guests have left, I'm quite exhilarated and even enjoy cleaning up a bit. I take the shower mat back into the bathroom and have a little chuckle to myself. Soon I'm lying in bed, awake, wide awake, but somehow happy.

Birthday encore

A gust of wind blows Manú in through the window and everyone jumps to the side. The coffee table splits in two.

"Tell us already," Rick calls from the kitchen.

"Yes, tell us," the others agree.

"Coward," Manú shouts angrily at me.

The old man from the shamanic journeys is sitting on

my left shoulder laughing out loud. *"You won't receive it, if you don't want to give it. Chase you through streets and squares it will. You cannot stop it. You must dare. Courage! Courage!"*

The house begins to sway and Manú asks, "Why do you want to keep it to yourself and stop the flow of yoga?"

Then she floats out the window on the shower mat and I wake up with a start before the house has had time to collapse. I'm breathing heavily. It's dark and quiet. A look at my phone tells me: 3:19. I have to get my bearings: Berlin, Friedrichshain, Weichselstrasse, my room, I'm lying in my bed. A look to the left tells me: alone. Good. Haha, so the comedian is still there too.

This thought in my head: I have to tell her. There's no way around it. If she thinks I'm crazy and breaks off contact with me, then that's how it has to be. But without opening up about these experiences, I don't see how we can communicate anymore, or more profoundly. Something would always be in the way.

Or should I wait and see how Manú reacts to the birthday meeting first? Maybe I should just ask her how she feels about dreams? That's good. I don't have to throw her right in the deep end. That's good.

I guess I fell asleep again then, because the next time I look at my phone, it's 8:59. The sparrows in the tree outside my bedroom window immediately remind me of last night's plans. It looks like I'll be arranging a meeting with Manú again very soon – I have to.

THE INNER UNIVERSE – AN UNKNOWN-FAMILIAR WORLD

Revelation

One day not long afterwards

Hey.
Feel like breakfast?

Hey back.
Feel like breakfast in the woods?

Confirm. I'll find something and send you the coordinates.

Then I'll take care of the survival pack.

The next morning, after what feels like an eternity, the train stops in Straußberg and we begin our march to the lake. Manú is carrying a woven basket stuffed to the brim. My backpack is pretty full too.

She peers over at me. "I just realised we're acting out a famous scene from a fairytale."

"I don't want to think about that image for too long," I respond.

"Okay."

"Although," I offer tentatively, "fairytales... that reminds me. What do you think about dreams?"

"I wouldn't exactly say its a hobby of mine, but yeah, I dream every now and again – even at night."

If this conversation gets too silly, I'll never get to the point. But somehow the words that would be capable of shifting the conversation in another direction won't come out.

"Wonderful weather for a picnic in the forest, I think."

"Yep." Manú whistles away to herself, the basket hooked onto her left arm, which brings the image of Hansel and Gretel to my mind again. My internal commentator offers me suggestions of ways to escape. I ignore him.

A short while later, a fallen tree and two tree stumps provide the setting for all our food and of course, coffee. We also have a full view of the lake from here. The excitement inside me is just as big as the emptiness in the place where there are normally words waiting to be used in conversation. But then the universe notices my predicament and sends me some help. Well, it's more like being given a push off the 10-metre diving board when you've been standing at the edge for way too long.

"I feel," says Manú, "like you have something you want to get off your chest, right?"

The vista of the lake is spread out before us. I feel a shudder go through my body.

My eyes dart back and forth between two boats and then comes the final push from the diving board.

"After 10 seconds, it's a yes, even without words."

She's got me.

"So, go on." Manú makes herself comfortable in her feel-good lotus position, takes a bread roll in her left hand and her coffee in the right. Then she looks at me expectantly.

I take a deep breath. "I had this dream a while ago. I met a man in it. In a fairytale you might call him a wiseman."

"A wiseman?" Manú seems surprised.

"Recently we had that idea, that idea with the ego. So like, visiting it."

"Yep, I remember."

"Well, so this dream was exactly about that. It was so clear, like nothing I've ever experienced, the way I spoke to this wiseman about my inner universe and, you know, what's going on there. And he was all mysterious about the ego."

"What did he say about it?"

"Nothing very specific unfortunately. I should meditate, then I'll find out more."

"Very interesting, I've got to say. And, did you meditate?"

"You remember Eric, from my birthday party?"

"Yep, the funny guy who gave you the teddy?"

Well, he's not really that funny, but it's true about the teddy – unfortunately.

"Exactly, him. He works with shamanic journeys in his therapy work and did it with me once."

"You went on journeys with him?"

"Figuratively speaking, yes."

"I know, I know, it's powerful stuff," Manú remembers. "I knew someone who used to do that kind of thing too." She looks at the ground as she says this, but I'd better not ask why.

"I did five journeys in the last three weeks."

"You did what? Five? If it even worked a tiny bit the way I imagine, then I'm amazed that you're sitting here so normally in front of me." When she says 'normally', she gestures some inverted commas with her coffee cup and bread roll.

"What's normal anyway? I didn't sleep so well the last few nights and yesterday I had a full-on nightmare."

"Well, there you go."

"It got a bit crazy in the shamanic journeys, because the information was always formulated in some weird kind of code. Statements a bit like laws, ground rules, there was even some talk about an energy structure. He talked about a universe."

Manú takes a bite of her roll as if she's being remote controlled. A leaf of lettuce falls out unnoticed. Her coffee cup is hanging so lopsided that the coffee is almost spilling out over the side. In the meantime, I've calmed down a lot and now I'm pretty excited about my own story.

"Go on," she says.

"He was talking about these entities that carry out tasks and in return harvest energy."

"Harvest?"

"Yeah, exactly, harvest. Although he talked about stealing too."

"Stealing what?"

"Well, the energy."

"From who?" asks Manú.

"No idea. There are also principles like 'more', 'wanting', 'having'. And then he says something like: *...and that always refusing as true too...*"

"What's that supposed to mean?" Manú wrinkles her brow.

"Maybe a not-wanting, not-having or losing something? It also sounds a bit like refusing the kinds of situations where I lose something. Right?"

Manú thinks, nods and then shakes her head. There seems to be an intense discussion going on inside her, which gives me a little break from talking.

"Those could be principles of the ego, couldn't they?"

I shrug.

"To me it sounds like our society's mantra: more and more and more," she adds.

"I mean, I did ask about the ego, so it does make sense that it was about that. And if I untangle the weird statements, then it does kind of fit."

"Wow, that's really interesting," she suddenly bursts out. "Messages from the other side, communicated by Tom Millar. And the way you're talking about it so realistically, you could make a public appearance."

"I'll talk to my manager about it. Let's see if I have any space in my schedule."

"Good one." She gives me a thumbs up and then asks: "Is there any more?"

"There is more," I announce, exhilarated by her enthusiasm.

"It is the grasping we require to appease the pain and yet the source all has. It is the opposition that reveals the things. Yet they can only manifest from unity."

"But how were you able to remember all this?" asks Manú with amazement.

"That's the unbelievable part. It's just there. I wrote it down straight away. But what's crazy is, I remember every detail, every word he said."

"Now that's what I call connected to whatever source it is." As she speaks, Manú looks into her coffee cup and I assure her that this is no coffee-grain fortune-telling I'm talking about here. As usual, she's quick off the mark and answers: "This look is more about the very earthly question of more coffee."

Then she considers: "Could what you just said maybe have something to do with non-duality?"

"Non-duality?" But my thoughts are slowly drifting elsewhere, while Manú excitedly tells me that they talked about oppositions in her yoga teacher training once. Things like cold/hot, up/down, love/hate may be opposite to each other, but also belong together somehow.

At the same time, I feel the part of my revelation that has kept me awake the last few nights more than anything I've said already coming closer. But my throat is so dry I can't get a word out. I say something to at least imply that there's more and – how could it be otherwise – Manú jumps on board straight away: "And what?"

"The last time I encountered the wiseman, it was about a kind of action without any connection to human beings. He was talking about faith, about waking and sleeping faith and that both are rooted in the inner universe."

"Sleeping faith?"

"I guess it's something like blind faith. So not just running after an idea without understanding the deeper meaning of what you're doing."

"A bit like at Christmas with the Christmas tree and no one knows why?" asks Manú.

I nod. "It's so crazy. If one of my friends told me something like this, I'd be sure they'd lost their mind. But on the journeys it feels so real and logical. Completely nuts."

I scratch behind my right ear and correct my sitting position unnecessarily.

"Is there any more?"

"On the last journey, he came a bit closer once and put his hands on my shoulders. It really felt like that. And when I had pulled myself together again, he spoke: *The door you see, the path is for you alone. Being ready, falling, floating, being. Your step into the void, the path's beginning marked.*"

"I don't get anything. Which door? Do you have any idea?" asks Manú, which sends a shockwave through me that collides against the walls of my skull from the inside. That's probably what makes my face turn red.

"Do you need to cool off?" She points, completely serious, to the lake that's peeping out quietly from behind the reeds and bushes and has been listening to everything. I say no, but take a sip of coffee to calm myself.

"The door... how can I describe it?" Manú falls silent and looks at me.

"At our workshop, remember I went outside once, when Josua did the guided meditation with the tears. Do you remember – the one with the child?"

"Yep, I know."

"I just couldn't take it anymore, the fear that I would just burst into tears and everyone would be looking at me." Manú nods, but doesn't say anything.

"It seems I always come up against some door when I don't face it. At least that's how Josua explained it, when we talked alone."

"You told him about that openly? Wow."

"More like he got it out of me by asking questions, I'd say."

"He's good at that," Manú agrees. "And is it the same door this wiseman was talking about?"

"Yes. How can I say this?" I take a deep breath. "So, I have a problem, just... well, with showing myself physically that way. Especially when feelings are involved." Another wave of energy rushes through me and makes my hair stand on end.

Manú is sitting up straight, looking at me. "Why do you reject your body?" she asks cautiously.

"Well that's obvious, isn't it! Because, well, because I'm too fat."

"Oh, really?" Manú asks, seriously surprised.

What does she mean by that? I mean, she has eyes in her head, doesn't she?

"Anyway, it seems to be connected to feelings somehow. As soon as things get too sentimental, all I want is to get away."

"What does one thing have to do with the other?" Manú is sitting bolt upright, her head cocked a little to one side.

"Then I have the feeling I'm exposing myself, if I suddenly started crying. It's like really taking off my clothes. Completely naked, in front of everyone. And then I just have to get away from all that chaos."

"Now I understand…"

"What do you understand?"

"When we had our first yoga session, I wondered if I had done something wrong."

"No, of course not."

"You left so quickly."

I look at the ground. "Ever since the workshop, I can't stop thinking about all this stuff with my feelings and my body. Ever since, I've noticed the thing with wanting to get away. But it still happens."

"And do you really think you're too fat?" Manú asks again.

"Well, do you think this is normal?" I gesture at the outline of my body with my hands. Manú's face is all question mark. Even if she's only pretending, it calms me down a bit.

"And then I always get these eating frenzies. It's probably connected, Josua said." Another one of those waves of energy cascades through my system. I think: I'm lost, utterly and completely. But I haven't even said everything yet. I close my eyes.

"The wiseman, and this is what's so crazy, he also talked to me about it. *The hundred questions are the metal of the key, which to you will show what you are running from. The answer's force will open up your walls to you, it will.* I've gone over these two sentences so many times in my head and I always come up with the same conclusion." I glance over at Manú quickly.

"I think someone needs to ask me these hundred, well let's say a lot of questions and I should answer without holding back at all."

"What kind of questions are they?"

"No idea, all something to do with this running away, eating and stuff – I guess."

Manú thinks it over. "And who is this someone?"

I look at her.

"What? Me?"

"Well, all the things we've been talking about the last couple of weeks. Sometimes I wonder if we haven't known each other longer."

"In another life perhaps?" asks Manú quietly and looks at me.

"After all the stuff I've experienced in the last three weeks, it doesn't seem impossible to me now."

A smile creeps across her face.

"What I understood from the wiseman is that I will find a path to the truth of my answers and that this path leads to my inner universe."

"Your inner universe?" Manú repeats. "That sounds... big."

"Then he also said that everything that is revealed by these questions cannot be undone. There's still the risk that I won't like these truths. *Truth, pain, not being happy, to you will bring peace in life.*"

I look at her. There's no sign that she thinks I'm insane yet. She's sitting there completely normally – the way she always does.

After a longer pause, she suddenly says: "I've already noticed that expressing your feelings spontaneously isn't really your thing. I just didn't know how preoccupied you were with it."

"I only fully realised at the workshop. Or maybe also during the first conversations we had and when we did stuff together. Like with yoga. I never thought I'd do yoga."

"But that changed pretty quickly," Manú notes with satisfaction.

"You have no idea how much I..."

"I think so. I guess your friends weren't just acting surprised."

I have to laugh. "True, they were really shocked."

Silence for a moment.

"I have the feeling I'll know you inside out and upside down after these hundred questions," says Manú finally.

"Does that mean you'll do it?" I ask quietly. Something jolts through my system – as if I'd just touched an electric current.

"I don't want to run away anymore when emotions come

up or I have to take off my T-shirt," my voice suddenly blurts out courageously. "Anyway, I have no choice."

"What do you mean?"

"How are we supposed to talk about all this stuff if I keep avoiding my feelings – now, when it couldn't be clearer to me, after what the wiseman said?"

Manú nods. "It would be pretty weird to philosophise about the truth with your own closet full of skeletons."

"I'm also pretty sure that these questions…"

"A hundred questions!" Manú raises her index finger sternly.

"…that these HUNDRED questions can't be as bad as what I'm doing here right now. And I'm pretty sure it doesn't have to be exactly 100."

"Your confession you mean?"

"No. Dealing with myself and these feelings in a more relaxed way." With my next exhale, it seems the dam has burst. I enjoy it with a big gulp of coffee. Manú raises her cup in my direction and says: "Alright. I'm in. To around a hundred questions about your inner universe." As she agrees, our eyes meet unexpectedly, for several seconds, until my gaze shies away to a flower behind her.

CHAPTER 8

On a Journey

Where Am I and If Yes – Why?

The week after my lake picnic revelation just flew by. I felt so good. It seemed the world belonged to me and there were no plans for a first round of questions yet. Manú was away visiting friends and so another week passed before we could arrange to meet for a hike on a Sunday.

Life in Berlin always requires a bit of nature to balance it out now and again. And so we, or rather Manú, couldn't resist a good deal on a rental car. The result: we follow the sat nav of a bright yellow Mini Cooper in the direction of Himmelpfort. This little village, around an hour north of Berlin, is known as the official Santa Claus headquarters – at least for this part of Germany. Well, that's how I imagine the Santa Claus empire organigram anyway, considering they have global responsibilities.

After almost an hour, Manú parks the bright yellow Mini

between two huge luxury class Mercedes. We take one more look at this unusual trio and then turn off onto a path towards the lake. The forest smells woody. When we hear snatches of the water splashing against the sides of the boats, it seems like the lake is greeting us. "Where are all the people normally enjoying nature on walks, bikes and in boats?" my commentator voice wonders.

"Exactly what I wanted for this truly sunny Sunday," says Manú. "This peace and quiet is heavenly." Since the name of the village means 'heaven's gate', I think it fits pretty perfectly.

We're walking along the narrow path, close to the water, when Manú asks me out of the blue: "If you had to give the happiness you feel right now a mark on a scale from 1 to 100, what would it be?"

"The questions?" My pulse races and it would be much easier to give my fear a mark on the scale instead of joy.

"Maybe 35 percent."

"And do you feel sadness too?"

"Oh man, now we're getting down to business." We continue walking. "Maybe a little bit actually." I'm hot. I take this as a sign that there are only 98 questions left – or at least two less, if the 100 isn't the benchmark.

I'm just in the process of finding whoever is making that rapid knocking sound in one of the trees, when Manú interrupts my bird search and asks: "And why?"

"Why am I sad? I... well, I don't really know either. It's just like that sometimes."

"It's just like that sometimes," repeats Manú and then says nothing.

Did I answer the question, I wonder? Then Manú points to a group of trees not even 30 metres in front of us. As we approach, we make out some unusually large stones. They form a triangle in the middle of the group of trees. We enter the circle.

"How do you feel right now?" asks Manú. "And where do you feel it?"

I try to feel something, but I'm distracted by the stones and the trees.

"I think...I guess...I don't know."

"Can you smell that too?" asks Manú.

I close my eyes, take a deeper breath in and out, and then sniff in various directions. There's a fragrance that describes this 'sun day' so sweetly and gently in a way that no words could. Where are the blossoms that are effusing such magic?

"Maybe it's actually more than 35 percent happiness," I correct my answer from before, as I hear a quiet voice in my ear.

"*Welcome, the two,*" it says right beside me.

We cross a meadow. The stranger, an old man with some unusual headgear, walks ahead. Suddenly the green starts to take on a more ordered structure and the grass is now lining a widening path. It leads us to a kind of forecourt in the shape of a crescent moon in front of a remarkable sort of gate. The lawn disappears as it reaches the entrance.

The stranger stops. We're standing in front of an enormous gate, which starts to gently open as if moving by itself.

With an inviting hand gesture, he turns to face us. "*Do not look, let yourself see with the heart only, understand here you cannot, with your mind. In this you are now and you are no longer up there, in the head.*"

Why are we following him like tame, wide-eyed little bunnies? I ask myself.

"*Inside is the outside at the same time and only my world it is that I see. In the transition, both show themselves, face and not-face at the same time. Then it is not a boundary, if two are brave enough to enter.*"

Then he allows us to go ahead of him through the gate. I haven't had this much reverence and been this obedient since first class. Plus it's quite astonishing that Manú hasn't uttered a peep yet.

On the left, a tower reaches up into the sky, much higher than the wall in front of it. It almost looks like there's a house perched on top of it. Why am I only seeing the tower now?

Right behind this Tower, as I read on the sign above the entrance, there is a roundish, spiral-shaped building with no windows. Or wait. Are those openings at the upper edge? A sign at the beginning of the path lined with flowers that links the Tower with this snail house tells us it's the Archive.

"I can smell flowers again," says Manú, enthused.

It's true. "Where are we here?" I ask, but get no answer. A wide road opens out in front of us, which seems to lead through the entire inner part of whatever-this-is. Is that a white shimmer all over the surface of the road? But the stranger directs our attention to the right, to a neat and tidy park filled with bright colours.

"That's the Villa Park. Only the best ones live there. Dale Detective lives there, he knows his stuff."

"What?" I say astonished. "Suddenly you're talking completely normally."

"Normally? How normal or should I say unnormal do I normally talk?"

I turn around and am looking at two ears, which clearly belong to a kangaroo, almost as tall as my shoulders. I let out a scream and we, all three of us, jump back a step. I look, it looks, Manú looks.

"I'll take it from here. The Guardian has to get back to his gate."

Manú bursts out laughing. "So funny, a talking kangaroo."

"What's funny?" asks the kangaroo.

He hops ahead with purpose and seems to be more than ready to give us a tour. "Let's Get Going," like it says on his T-shirt.

"Wait a second," I protest. "First I want to know what's going on here?"

"Oh, sorry. Didn't even introduce myself. I'm Roo."

"Manú."

"Wait, wait, that's not what I mean," I interrupt. "I want to know where the hell we are?"

Roo scratches behind his right ear: "Well, you should

know that, you should. You registered, didn't you? So now I'm going to show you everything." He's already hopping ahead.

"Wait a minute!" I hurry after him. "Registered where?"

Manú is giggling away and I'm starting to feel a bit unwell around my stomach.

"Where indeed?" the kangaroo asks, bemused. "In you."

"In me? Just stop for a second. What do you mean, I registered us?"

"Questions about questions," says Roo and seems satisfied that this has answered everything.

I look at Manú, who just shrugs her shoulders and doesn't seem to share my confusion at all.

"Okay, one more time," says Roo. "This is the Villa Park. Dale Detective lives here, I'm sure you'll meet him."

"Who's Dale Detective?" I ask, "And why Villa Park?" But our hopping tour guide is already almost out of sight. He seems to have turned off to the left towards a large square. When we get closer, we see colourful forms surrounding the square. They look a bit like something painted by the artist Hundertwasser, although every shape only has one colour.

I want to keep going, but Manú holds me back by the rucksack.

"The kangaroo has to answer a few more questions for me," I say quickly.

"Do you remember? The questions? That's exactly what I just started. I think my questions brought us deeper into your inner world than you wanted," Manú realises.

"My inner world?" I look around, more confused. By now the kangaroo has returned and overhears me asking Manú why there's a kangaroo jumping around in my inner world.

"Well, because that's what you want," he says promptly.

I do remember a kangaroo stuffed animal from my childhood, but no, that can't have anything to do with it. I'm dreaming, that's for sure. The only weird thing is: how do I know I'm dreaming?

"Let's see what happens if we go with this Roo guy. It's pretty interesting, isn't it?"

I don't share Manú's spirit of adventure one bit, but I have to admit that I am curious. I wonder what else might happen here?

"What's the worst that can happen? You think that half-size kangaroo is going to kidnap us and take us away to some distant galaxy?"

I shake my head, more baffled at how relaxed Manú is about the situation than as an answer to her question.

"The market square here, you should really go when the market is marketing. You'd like it. Isn't boring. Promise. A few quanta and off you go."

"Quanta? What are quanta?" I ask.

"That's how you pay, if you're buying things," says the kangaroo briefly.

"So real money, only for here?" I ask.

"Quanta and particles. 100 particles make up a quantum."

"And where can one get these quanta?"

"Playing, doing something or just taking them from someone else. Everything in its own time. You'll figure it out." And then suddenly, he disappears behind a kind of house, which has a green shimmer. We try to keep up. We keep catching a glimpse of a piece of the high wall that we saw extend out on either side of the entrance gate.

"Does the wall go around everything that's happening?" Manú asks.

"Not 'a wall', but a not-wall is what that is. Doesn't divide and yet keeps things out."

"What's that? And what does the wall keep out?"

"Not 'the wall', but the not-wall. That's something else. It keeps the world of things out, the place where it comes from."

"Where we come from." I laugh. "What kind of a statement is that? Are we not in this world now?"

"Yes. Sure, you are. But not in the world of things, with us."

"Do you mean in Himmelpfort?" I ask, but Roo, unbothered, hops back onto the wide road with the white shimmer under its surface. We keep walking. Soon there is some glinting and sparkling on the right side. A huge green hill like half a football rises up behind it.

"Can you see the party strip?" The kangaroo points to the glittery field. "Everything fun, everything that helps you wind down – party – is here."

We follow Roo across a green filled with flowers. There's a sweet fragrance, like just before in the group of trees with the stones. The colours glow and a lovely warmth envelops us. In front of us and to the right, there are quite a lot of bushes. The spiky, dark leaves make the undergrowth seem a bit sinister. Some of them seem a bit withered. Then the meadow of flowers ends abruptly. Behind it a dense woods and those shrubs again.

"Seems like we can't get through. Let's go left. We must be able to see the road from somewhere," says the kangaroo to himself.

Briefly, the feeling creeps over me that I associate with hiking trips, when someone always knows a short-cut that later on is renamed "lost". The kangaroo hops ahead, looking left and right. He scratches his belly and behind his left ear. Then he stops.

"What are those bushes?" I ask.

"All that belongs to the Garden Fields. This meadow does too. And underneath us, there are loads of different q-u-a-l-i-t-i-e-s." As he says this, he taps the ground several times with his paw.

"The character of the quaaa-ties, or whatever they're called, allows certain plants to grow. And others grow over there and different ones again there. They all have their own information. It keeps you healthy and helps with work."

"Do you make tea out of them or do you eat the flowers?"

The kangaroo looks at me. "But there are no things here. All energy! All information! Your information." As he says this, he pushes me gently with his foot, while balancing himself on his tail.

"What you call happiness is energy." Roo hops happily back and forth. Suddenly he pulls his ears back and bares his teeth fiercely. Manú and I take a step back and the kangaroo says angrily: "This is energy too. Nothing more than energy." And then just as quickly, he's back to hopping back and forth happily.

I look at the meadow of flowers and feel that warm, happy feeling again. Then I look over to the bushes and feel a sense of uneasiness, even a small stabbing feeling around my stomach. Staring at the tall trees, I get the sudden urge to rip them out of the ground. When I direct my attention back to the meadow of flowers, joy immediately spreads through me, even a smile across my face.

I ask the kangaroo whether no one looks after the garden here and whether this thick undergrowth and these dry bushes are deliberate. He thinks, scratches his belly again and behind his left ear, and then shrugs.

"I think there were once fewer plants in the gardens. Is it meant to be like that?" He ponders again. "And does anyone do anything with this stuff? You'll have to ask in the office. Maybe someone there knows. And here it is!"

The kangaroo jumps up and, with a backwards somersault, lands on his hindlegs. Then he leaps into the bushes in front of us and all we can hear is some rustling.

Manú looks at me. "I find this kangaroo extremely entertaining."

My face is getting hot again. Then we follow the rustling through the ferns, past little bushes and through a piece of forest with tall, large-leafed trees. The kangaroo is swinging happily in circles around a tree.

"The road is there again!" he calls out cheerfully. The whitish shimmer is now glowing even more intensely than before at the entrance.

"Where does this, I guess, not-a-road lead?" Manú asks the kangaroo.

"The Potential Gate is up ahead there." He points to the right and draws lots of curves with his paw, which I guess we'll encounter before the road reaches its destination.

"Next question: what's the Potential Gate? Right?"

I sigh and nod.

"There's not much going on around there. I've never been there myself. Sounds a bit boring, so I don't care."

"Is it the exit?" Instead of giving us an answer, the kangaroo signals us to cross the road by waving his tail in little circles. As soon as we do, we hear a rustling in the bushes on the other side.

"If it's all about energy here, then that kangaroo clearly has some great batteries in his belly," says Manú and tries to keep up with this hopping Roo.

I find it more unbelievable that this Roo can't give a clear answer to a single one of my questions. In that moment, the gardens transform once again. Herbs, vegetables and again meadows of flowers astound me once more. Manú seems to be quite bowled over too, which is evident in her wide-eyed stare.

"Someone is definitely looking after the gardens here," she asserts. Some of the beds are blooming gloriously. Others seem to need a bit of watering. But overall this part seems to be well tended to.

Countless thoughts and feelings come and go as I walk among the beds. Slowly I begin to understand how the information influences my feelings and my motivation to want to do something specific, or even determines it. At the bushes with the spiky leaves, I felt a strong urge to get away, here I feel joy. All of a sudden, I wish I could play squash with Manú again. When I tell her that, she looks at me in disbelief. Then it's just me who feels this? Does this all really only have to do with my inner world? And Manú is really with me everywhere here? A shudder runs down my spine.

Then I have to keep her away from the dangerous areas. And we only ended up here, because she asked those questions? This is too much, just too much.

"I think I would remember a kangaroo who is moving away from us already at great speed." Manú pulls me back out from my thoughts. Once again, at a light gallop, we try to catch up with him.

"This here," Roo points to a structure right in front of us, "is the Parliament and the Department of Science and, and…" Again he scratches his belly and behind his left ear.

"…and well, lots of us live here," he finally says.

"The green guy over there is the Controlletti. I'm sure you'll meet him in the Office. The orange guy is my friend, the Terrier. The other orange guy is the Cake King, the red guy is The Flaming Sword and the light yellow one, that's the Quiet One."

"And what about that multi-coloured one over here?" Manú asks.

"He calls himself Mister Public Relations, Mr PR for short. He actually managed to make himself look completely colourful. He's always networking, he knows all the right people. He used to just be pink, pink, pink. He's cool and sometimes he really gets on some people's nerves. Because he's really great fun and is always ready with his famous 'Yeah, let's do it!'"

"Oh," notes Manú, "another one with an amazing battery."

I shrink back, because the kangaroo heard that.

"Yeah, sure," he says amused, "a few of us are generally in good form. Like my job, works out well, is fun and I always get lots of energy." He dances on one paw circling to the right as he says this. Then he changes direction for another full circle.

"What do you have to do here to get energy?" Manú asks.

I feel I should step in. "Oh no! I'm sure you don't need any extra energy!"

The kangaroo and Manú look at each other conspiratorially. To be on the safe side, I change the subject before Manú starts hopping too. "So what's the Parliament?" I ask.

"Kind of the basic underlying mood. Whoever there's the most of has the say. And that's where our basic energy comes from."

"Basic energy?" I ask, a bit annoyed. How the hell should I know what that is?

Slowly, I start to suspect that I'm coming face to face with some of my not-so-lovable flaws. I always assumed that my friends knew them as well as I thought I did, and I guess there were some complaints that I ignored. Did Roo notice that? Maybe he's talking through me then? Is HE my commentator voice? Oh God, no! Oh man, I think I'm starting to lose my mind.

"How do you communicate with each other anyway?" Manú asks the kangaroo in the meantime.

"With the frequencies of course!" The kangaroo seems to be surprised at this question. One of his ears is sticking out to the side.

"Well, everyone has a frequency. That's why there are so many colours. You get it?"

We shake our heads in sync. The kangaroo looks at Manú, then at me, then back at Manú again, involuntarily shaking his head at the same time.

"Okay, to put it another way. If there's something to do, like for me. Then I get a message from the Tower."

"How do you get the message – on a phone?"

"Don't be ridiculous. It just makes sense for me when they use my frequency. Then I just need the file and off I go and get some energy."

"The file?"

"Yes. You'd better ask in the Office – or in the Archive. I'm sure there's a tour there."

"Office, Tower, Archive." Manú nods thoughtfully and looks at me with pursed lips and wide eyes.

"Sounds like we might be here a while."

"I'm definitely not staying here longer than I need to," I complain again – whoever I'm complaining to, since the two of them have already gone on ahead.

I raise my eyebrows and my shoulders and wonder if the idea of me coming here was really considered properly by the "staff".

"Over there," the kangaroo points to the right and

signals to something behind the structures in light pastel colours. "That's the Factory."

"Does this wide range of colours come from your drug period?" asks Manú. She bursts out laughing, but tries to pull herself together straight away. It seems she compensates her feeling of being overwhelmed with humour. I make an exception and let the comment slide, but answer no just for the sake of order.

"And what's this Factory?" asks Manú.

"That's where the energy of the IU is managed, produced, distributed. Really important. I work there too."

"IU?" I ask.

"We say that for short. Means i-n-n-e-r u-n-i-v-e-r-s-e. The Guardian came up with it."

"The guy who brought us here?" asks Manú.

The kangaroo nods.

Now I realise. That wiseman on those shamanic journeys was the Guardian too. He also mentioned an inner universe. How is this possible? How can this really exist?

I suddenly notice an almost white line snaking along the garden fields, through Roo's legs and disappearing into the bushes behind him.

"What was that?" I ask.

Roo looks down and jumps a little to the side. "The Earth Cable." I start to ask a new question, but the kangaroo blocks my question by holding up his paw and looks to the side: "Don't ask me. I don't know. Something to do with the Potential Gate. Sometimes energy comes from there in any case. But who knows exactly how it works?"

I just accept this and give up asking any more questions, I'm not getting any satisfying answers anyway.

"Thanks for your understanding," the kangaroo adds in an exaggerated formal tone and then immediately jumps ten metres ahead, before we can get going too. We follow at our usual brisk pace – no actually, running.

On the other side of the road, the "party strip" appears again and Manú feels compelled to make a comment: "Looks a bit empty."

"A sign that this has nothing to do with me, right?" I retort.

"A sign that there's nothing going on here," Manú corrects me.

"The Great Parade Day was the last big event," the kangaroo notes.

"What day?"

"Parade Day. Everything's happening then."

"Maybe your birthday?" concludes Manú.

"You're saying my birthday is a big deal for me?"

Manú gives me a quick thumbs-up, but is already hurrying after the kangaroo, who has turned off into a meadow on the right.

"No way," I try to set things straight.

Welcome – Because no choice is also a yes

Then suddenly the Tower that we had previously only noticed out of the corner of our eye appears before us. It looks like there's a house sitting on top of it. It has rows of many windows. It seems to be brighter behind these windows.

"That's where we're going now," says the kangaroo, following my gaze.

Manú wants to ask about that green hill as round as a football behind the empty party strip. A castle-like dark structure looms on its summit, which seems to be at around the same height as the tower house. But the kangaroo has already disappeared into the Tower and we follow inside, and up the stairs, until a bright room opens up to us. The kangaroo is waiting at an open door, tapping his tail lightly on the ground.

I wonder what's going to happen next?

For the first time, Manú refuses when I offer her to go ahead. And so, I go cautiously into the bright-looking room.

"A warm welcome, welcome, welcome!" a high-pitched male voice sings to greet me. A stately figure in a brightly coloured jacket is striding swiftly towards me. He shakes my hand with both hands and comes unnecessarily close to do this. Because of this, I can't avoid noticing the pearls of sweat on his brow.

"An applause for our guests," he calls out loudly and much too closely to my left ear. There is some slightly unenthusiastic clapping and cheering for us.

A dark moustache graces the face of a tall, thin man wearing a suit. His thin lips are not so noticeable under his neat moustache, but his critical look meets my eye for a few seconds, before he scurries over to Manú.

The man in the brightly coloured jacket speaks proudly and ceremoniously to us: "This is the famous Tower Office, the information headquarters of the inner universe, our wondrous world. Thanks to our wonderful team," he gestures behind him to the crowds standing in orderly rows, "we have set up a highly efficient and modern information system, which is available day and night for your needs. I'd like to take the opportunity…"

My gaze and my thoughts drift to the man with the neat moustache, who seems to have to make an effort to hide his uneasiness about the situation. Another "wonderful" member of the team smirks a little as he rolls his eyes and I notice another looking stressed and massaging his forehead. The speaker, in contrast, is effusing euphoria: "…to thank everyone here for their outstanding work. Our two visitors will have the opportunity to admire our work. All the staff are happy to answer any questions you have. Don't hesitate. Ask, ask, ask. Don't just stand on the sidelines, no, get involved!"

He opens his arms and a seam audibly bursts. Several members of the team can be heard clearing their throats.

"Welcome," he cries once more. "Welcome to our family. Thank you for coming and you, dear friends," he turns around to the team once again, "for listening."

A round of applause ensures that Mr PR, as I now read on the little sign on his lapel, will not continue his speech. One by one the others come over to us and introduce themselves.

The man with the moustache calls himself Controlletti,

as he tells us. He will explain the office work to us tomorrow in more detail. The Analyst introduces himself and asks Manú straight out what she liked best about Mr PR's speech. Manú looks at me for help. "He's very motivated," she says finally.

"Yes, that's true," a small man with a soft voice answers. He greets us briefly, but then he's gone again. The Analyst informs us: "That was the Perfectionist."

I have no idea what's going on anymore and wonder how we're supposed to find our way out of this situation back home. Everyone here knows about our arrival, but how could they? How come I don't know anything about it?

I ask Manú: "How are we going to get out of here again?"

"I don't think we can right now," she decides matter-of-factly. Then, full of curiosity, she pulls someone aside and before long, she's deep in conversation. I wander extremely aimlessly through the room, unable to orientate myself. Is this really my world, my inner universe? Why does this suddenly feel so real? Then it occurs to me that maybe it's not so bizarre. On the shamanic journeys, the wiseman, or the Guardian, had already implied something like this.

Deeply lost in my thoughts, suddenly someone pulls at my arm. "Hey, come on." Roo jumps ahead. "You've met the Guardian. He knows about the not-a-wall." He pushes me through the room with purpose.

"You're the stranger from before and the wiseman from the journeys."

He nods kindly. "*The a-not, like wall, street, form it gave. You want to know more?*"

"I don't get the thing with the 'a-not' and the kangaroo couldn't tell me anything about it either. What does it mean?

"*Created dual, think first, manifestation in things follows. You see in form the one, born from nothing. What is sown in thought, later bears large tangible fruit. Although nothing is in every beginning, it is part of everything for eternity.*"

With that he puts on his hat and disappears among the "staff", as Mr PR called them.

Suddenly I'm bombarded with questions from the others. As if I belonged here, that's what it feels like. Time passes. Where's Manú anyway?

"Hey, there you are," someone says excitedly behind me.

Manú is standing there with at least four others.

Completely unexpectedly, and only after much protest and a lot of peer pressure I could not defend myself against, I finally agree to stay a bit longer.

Roo brings us to an area that has an unbelievably relaxed atmosphere. A temple of peace. Several areas seem to be connected to each other like a labyrinth. Manú has followed a red glow that is coming out of one the little cosy corners.

"I'll take that one." She lets herself sink down onto the soft floor. I choose the green corner. Here too the floor is as soft as velvet.

"Can you hear me?" I ask into the nothingness.

"Yes."

"Am I sleeping in a dream now?"

"Is that possible?" she asks back.

"Don't know."

"I talked to the Guardian," it suddenly occurs to me.

No answer. I try hard to figure out what he said. No chance. Then in my mind I see the team standing in front of me again. Somehow, some of them are familiar to me. Like Controlletti. I have to smirk when I remember a situation from before: "Funny that the Hectician knocked a glass off the table when you wanted to shake hands."

I hear a faint "Yeeeeah…" make its way over to me.

"Who was that guy who disappeared again straight away?"

"Don't know, with water…"

"What did you say"

"Yes."

"Okay then, good night."

CHAPTER 9

As If There Were No Tomorrow

Just listen

The next morning, Manú is suddenly standing in front of me. They want to show us their work in the Office today, but as far as I know not right now.

"Are you receiving yet?"

"Ask up there in the Tower Office," I respond, but I signal that I'm ready to listen. "Go for it."

"I can only barely imagine what this must be like for you, me being here in your inner world in such an open and vulnerable way. The experiences here..." she pauses for a moment and swallows loudly. "It's more than just a crazy dream. It touches me just as much. It seems that a lot of it resonates with my inner world. Like the thing with the kangaroo. I think I have a character like that in me too. A squirrel, I think." She takes a deep breath: "Only I can decide if I let it show or not." And a little more quietly, she adds: "Well, it's kind of unfair."

Her forehead catches my eye, where two lines appear and then disappear again. It's good to hear this after all the confusion and chaos yesterday.

"We have to find out how to get out of here again," I say.

"But isn't it unbelievably interesting getting to know your inner world so close up?"

"Definitely interesting. But do I really want this?"

"Now we're here. You should find out."

"I never planned it this way, with the questions. I thought you'd just ask me a few things about my life and we'd talk the way we usually do. But now: look around. This is completely nuts! Where have we ended up?"

"I have an idea. Let's do something. It's called checking in."

I look at her puzzled. Why checking in? Having only just woken up, I see no link at all to checking into a hotel. But before I can ask, this seems to be heading in the direction of 'this is how we'll do it'.

"We tell each other about our thoughts and feelings, how we're doing, experiencing all this here."

"That won't take long," I reply. "Pure chaos. Or what do you mean?"

"You listen as openly as possible, without judgement. Whatever comes up, you don't argue with it or offer unsolicited comments. What's said is just there. Then we'll know how the other is doing when we're wandering around this place later. When I'm finished, I'll thank you for listening. Then it's your turn."

I think about it. To my own surprise, "Okay, let's try

it," stumbles out of my mouth. Well, what have I got to lose, if my life story is hanging off every tree here anyway.

"Who's gonna start?" I ask.

"The person who suggested it."

"That's you."

Manú sits in lotus facing me. She inhales deeply.

"Yesterday was unbelievable. It was so surprising and new for me. I realised that in situations like this I tend to see everything as funny. I had a lot of fun. Only later I understood that it's about your inner world, your, well, i-n-n-e-r u-n-i-v-e-r-s-e, as the kangaroo said.

"Anyway that made me sad, when I realised how unbelievably funny I thought this all is. It reminded me of your ego story, when I couldn't stop laughing. That was the same.

"I saw so many things yesterday that I recognise from my own life: the kangaroo, the dark, spiky bushes and the fragrant meadows. I think I have that in me too."

Manú pauses for a moment.

"And then I realised that I wasn't laughing about the kangaroo and you, but about myself. About my life."

A tear runs down Manú's cheek. A second follows quickly. My throat feels really dry and I can clearly hear my heartbeat.

"I woke up with this feeling of sadness this morning and I just want to be with that today, just like that. Thanks for listening."

Manú sniffles a little, wipes away her tears and smiles sheepishly. I'm sitting up poker-straight and motionless in front of her, I keep looking at her as if she's still speaking.

Then I take a deep breath too.

"I feel a bit of confusion and maybe a bit of panic growing in me. It's so unbelievable what's happening here. I keep thinking I'm dreaming and that I'll wake up soon.

"At the same time, I can't ignore that everything here has something to do with my life, somehow. How did I get here? And how can I get away again? Someone who looks like a kangaroo calls this my i-n-n-e-r u-n-i-v-e-r-s-e. Am I crazy? And if this all has something to do with me, how long has it existed? Why don't I know anything about it?"

My head is spinning a little.

"No idea how this is supposed to go on, how I'm supposed to meet these parts of me. I mean even in the Office there were enough, enough... what were they? Me's, its or should I say staff, there? I don't even know if I should be casual with them or more official. Oh God, this is nuts. All I want is it to stop."

There's silence for a moment.

"Thanks, I'm finished."

"How did that feel?" Manú asks.

I'm amazed. Subjects like this so early in the morning. But who knows whether it really is early in the morning? Maybe there is no next day? I have no sense of time at all. We left our phones in the car because we were doing a Sunday digital detox. Great idea!

Anyway, it's unusual: this check-in, someone just listening, giving me the feeling I can just be there and just somehow the whole thing. Slowly the thumping in my chest gets softer. It feels good.

"It's okay with me," I say finally. "Let's take a quick look at the Office and then find the way back."

Manú nods half-heartedly and I immediately start preparing for our 'departure'. I pack a smile into my rucksack too. Why not?

How it thinks when it thinks

There's a knock and the kangaroo asks if we're ready for the Office. The quiet drumming of his tail on the ground suggests that it's more of an urgent order than a question.

"We'll be right there," I call out and quickly whisper into Manú's ear: "The funny comments are usually fine. It's good to have something to laugh about. Then all this madness is easier to handle."

It's all go at the Office. Mr Controlletti comes straight over to us and greets us warmly, but officially: "Welcome to the Tower Office. Now I'll show you what we do here. Please follow me." The kangaroo is more than ready to lead us around, but is stopped by Mr Controlletti: "Oh, thanks very much. I'll do it myself. I'll let you know if I need your help." He hops away without comment.

Controlletti makes a grand gesture signalling to the back part of the office and goes on ahead.

"Did he really comb his moustache?" I ask Manú very

quietly. She quickly looks in the opposite direction – trying to stop herself from bursting out laughing. So we continue in silence, just to be on the safe side.

Desks, some tidy, others not so tidy, coffee cups – no surprise there. There are – let's call them staff – standing, sitting and walking around, who nod to us. It seems as though lots of them are coordinating something. Are they working on stand-by?

One desk looks bigger. It's covered in papers, spilling over the edge in a huge irregular shape. All the paper is only being held together by the coffee cups on top of it and piles of folders. In the middle of this mountainous island of paper, someone is beavering away. Mr Controlletti looks disdainfully over and immediately away again. I'm almost sure that it was that diligently hard-working fellow who almost spilled water all over Manú yesterday, if that saviour all dressed in white had not intervened with his magical hand. "Pretty hectic here." Manú is looking at the mountains of paper in front of us. The rustling stops and a small figure with tousled hair looks up.

"Yes-yes, always lots to do. Wish you-wish you an interesting tour of the Office. Sorry, I-I have to get back to work."

He squints at the mess of paper and then we hear the rustling again.

"Hey," asks Manú, "does he have his shirt buttoned wrong?" I nod without looking at Manú. Now I have to try to control my laughter.

When we arrive at the windows, the Controlletti begins: "The Tower Office is our headquarters."

Does he know the world out there, I wonder? "Out there is the world of things. We get information from them."

Manú has stepped closer to the window and is looking out with interest. It looks like there's a thick fog.

"We look for familiar events, dangers, sources of energy there."

"What kind of energy sources?" I ask.

"Usually it's people. They motivate us to act. Where there are people, there's also energy and then we get to work."

"How does that work?" I ask, while Manú tries to discern something 'out there'.

"Files, filled with memories, are activated. We compare and assess. Urgency and intensification play a role and then the job goes out to the corresponding action frequency."

Manú looks at me. I shrug my shoulders, which matches her this-is-all-double-Dutch-to-me face.

"Could you maybe explain that again, sir?" Manú asks cautiously.

"Yes. But I must say something else first. I'm Con and no one says sir around here." As he says this, he bows slightly in Manú's direction.

"Manú." She makes a little curtsey.

"Tom," I say quietly. This Con definitely knows who I am. Whatever.

Con Controlletti now begins to explain his work in precise detail.

"All the emotis get their jobs assigned by the Tower Office."

Although I'm also interested in what he meant by intensification, action frequency and jobs, first I just ask: "What do you mean by emoti?"

"We are emotis."

"Why emotis?"

"Why are other beings humans, dogs or goats?" he asks in return.

"Does it come from emotion?" asks Manú.

"Who knows?" Con answers Manú.

"E-motion as in energy in movement! Makes sense, right?" Manú looks over at me quickly and waits in vain for the coin to drop with me, because I'm already on to the next question: "What did you mean before with intensification?"

Con briefly smooths his moustache: "Every file causes a more or less strong intensification. There are three stages. Do you want to know how they're produced?" Now he's just fondling his moustache.

"It has to do with danger and how memories are stored when they were created. Some memories in the files are intensified, others aren't."

"Those kinds of memories are more important than others then. Pedi knows more about how that works. He works over in the Archive."

I nod, only half-satisfied, which inspires Con to suggest sending us to Pedi for the afternoon.

"Oh thanks. But we might already be gone by then," I inform him.

"Gone?" Con looks at us astonished.

"What was I talking about?" Con thinks aloud. "We have the memories in the files and we compare them with new information that we discover in the world of things."

"And how does that work?" Manú asks.

"We watch, listen, touch, use our taste buds and smell some things. If memories are awakened by new information, then we check and process that: compare information, assess the situation and work out action suggestions," he says. "Take a look at this."

"Action suggestions are especially important when the file status has changed."

"You just said memories are activated with the new information. What did you mean by that?" asks Manú.

"Everything around here is based on energy and it gets to us with various frequencies. Information is also energy."

"Ha!" I suddenly burst out. Both of them are startled and look at me.

"I once had this dream about information and how matter is created from it."

I look expectantly at Manú, who obviously didn't file that in her archive.

"Information is directed energy," I remember.

"If by directed you mean one single frequency, then that's true," says Con.

"If we get new information with the same frequency, like memories, then these get activated straight away. That makes us aware of the situation. There are fundamental frequencies too that are always around when there's a certain situation."

"Like danger?" asks Manú.

Con nods.

"So what happens after you've done your work?" I ask.

"Different frequencies are associated with the various results, which are then assigned to the emotis who share this frequency spectrum. And then they do their job – hopefully," adds Con.

He looks at me, then Manú, then back at me. He nods thoughtfully.

"An example, we need an example."

Manú waits in anticipation.

"The file status changed with your first yoga session recently." He looks at me. "yoga is interesting and is fun. You might do more. It's cool, etc. That was added. Before it was more..." he looks at Manú and says carefully, "a different opinion. The file is also 'emotionally intensified', which is what this one mark means."

"How?" I blurt out.

"The intensification comes from the gymnastics-on-the-high-bar situation, back in school."

Con really knows a lot about my life. What's next?

Manú is listening intently. Con seems to be in a very carelessly chatty mood, because he finds it by no means inappropriate to add that Manú's gentle and touching ways attracted so much attention in the Office that there was a basic level intensification for that new information too.

Only then does he realise his monologue is maybe a bit too open and, in my opinion, over-the-top, and quickly changes the subject. I'm getting hot, really hot actually!

"I'd like to tell you about the action frequencies now," he says after a short pause.

I nod, relieved, although I hardly understand anything anymore.

"Does that have to do with the jobs that go out to the emotis?" asks Manú.

"Correct." Con continues as we go over to the windows that look out into this inner universe. Now we have a full view of what we saw from the ground yesterday: the Villa Park, the glittery party strip, the hill as round as a football with the sinister structure on top and the Garden Fields all the way in the distance.

"Every emoti has their own frequency. That means they only get information that fits with their spectrum of action. Each frequency can be recognised by its colour. That's why we're visible to you."

"The structures we saw on our walk yesterday," asks Manú, "are they those colours too?"

"Yes exactly. Those are the activation fields. Each emoti works in one. You'd probably say building or workplace. Everyone has their place here."

"And these places of activity, are they something like the centre of an emotion and I feel the activation exactly there?"

"The centre of an emotion?" repeats Con. "If you like, yes."

"That's fantastic!" she exclaims.

Con looks a little puzzled. "That's just the way it works."

"In my yoga training, we were supposed to direct our

attention to the centre of an emotion, learn to feel deeper into that place. Perceive how the energy moves out from there. I never saw it as an activity, but as something that kind of contracts or pulsates."

Manú is completely beside herself. "I didn't know that I was watching you work when I did that."

"Not necessarily us, but our colleagues in your world," says Con.

"Every emoti tries, following their own pattern, to cause reactions and influence actions. The procedure of the way an emoti works is always the same though."

"Stop, wait a second," I say. "Don't you define the procedure with your recommendations?"

"Look, up till now whenever you talked about your opinion of yoga, you basically always rejected it, you expressed that with words and convictions. And yet you spoke about it a bit differently and acted a bit differently in each situation. The basic action followed a model or checklist. Acting a certain way in situations comes from our recommendations."

"Is the file the model?" I ask.

"No. The file serves to interpret the situation, the model is more like the basic architecture of the structure."

I puff out my cheeks and look over at Manú. She signals to me that I'd better not.

"If language is necessary, there's a microphone we can use. Then it's a bit like the emotis are giving orders. Each one in their own way. Does that make sense to you?" asks Con.

"I do know the feeling of sometimes being controlled by other forces very well," I admit.

"I'm interested in the thing with the microphone. Who speaks into it?" It reminds me of my not-so-beloved commentator voice.

"Anyone can speak. Depending on who's active at the moment and who also uses language for their work."

"So it's not just one, but many commentators?" I realise, shocked. This seems to be a new discovery for Manú as well. She's scratching her head for the third time now.

I puff out my cheeks again. "So, understand everything?" comments Manú pointedly.

Shaking my head, I release the air out of my mouth.

"Energy is attracted to the emoti in exactly the same frequency, at the same level that the emoti is active."

"And that's the payment for their action," notes Manú.

I'm still nodding as if I'm interested, but I can't take in any more information or new terms. So I thank him and then admit that I'm impressed, speechless and confused.

"I feel the same," I hear Manú say – not very typical of her, actually.

Con is sure that bit by bit, it will become more understandable for us. "It's a question of looking. We'll do it every day. I'm sure you'll notice the procedures more from now on." With a somewhat stiff bow, he says goodbye and then he's gone.

We go back to our sleeping nooks and I haven't enjoyed a midday power nap as much in a very long time.

Later Manú and I are sitting together. "Tell me," she begins, "did Con mean the kangaroo earlier when he was talking about chaos in the Office?"

"Don't know."

"Maybe that's why he was so frosty to Roo?"

"You mean there are problems here too?" I ask.

"Why not?"

"Please no! The world out there is so chaotic, don't tell me it's just as bad in here."

"As above so below, as left so right, as inside so outside."

We look at each other.

"The war in the mind is the source of all evil."

Memory management or just something to remember?

A short time later, we hear a rhythmic knocking.

"That must be the kangaroo," I guess.

"The Archive is waiting. I'll bring you there. Are you ready?"

His tail knocks audibly on the ground.

"We're right behind you," I call through the door. The knocking stops and when we come out, he's just turning his head back again. "Ha ha."

"We're ready," I say. He hops quickly ahead of us and we follow at a brisk pace until we get to the spiral-shaped structure.

Inside, a haggard little emoti, who formulates everything

extremely correctly, thanks the kangaroo kindly but firmly, and insists we don't need his help right now. The kangaroo hops away disappointed and we go further into the snail house. The small man walks ahead at a calm pace. There are shelves with files in various shapes and colours towering to the left and right of us. At least it looks like that, but somehow the whole ensemble seems strange, as if the files are slightly blurred. I rub my eyes. Manú looks at me. "Tired?"

"No, out of focus."

The small man laughs and says: "That's the connectedness."

"Connectedness?" I ask.

"Yes," he says and turns around to us, "I never introduced myself to you properly yesterday. Pedant." He offers Manú his hand and adds: "But people just call me Pedi, that's fine too."

"Manú," she says quickly.

With a deep breath and lagging what feels like years behind, I also introduce myself officially.

Pedi points to the shelves on both sides. "What you see here is the entire stored memory in the inner universe. Thoughts, fragrances, sounds, touches and everything in combination if needed."

"And a more or less strong intensification of them, if I understood correctly," I add.

"Yes, the intensification. Con already informed me that I need to clear up a few things for you. So let's just start with that, okay?"

"Yes, great. Let's solve the mystery right at the start," Manú says cheerfully.

Pedi thinks. "Intensification mainly comes from the early time, so from the beginnings."

"You mean my childhood?" I ask.

"That must have been a very exciting time for you all, right?" asks Manú.

"Hardly any emotis, few memories and countless unfamiliar situations every day. Most of them were intensified. These days, intensification doesn't happen very often. Unless…" Pedi looks at us from the side, "love drugs are involved."

Whaaat? Why did he mention that now, I wonder?

"What's different then?" Manú wants to know.

"All kinds of things are given intensification. It's terribly hard work, for example, when a shower mat is given a double intensification, although it makes no sense. I said double!" Pedi shows two fingers. "Not easy."

"Why do the shelves have different colours?" I ask.

Manú looks around. Her facial expression reveals that, firstly, she hadn't noticed this and that, secondly, now she wants to know too – which really calms me down. With a knowing look on his face, Pedi declares himself ready to play the game with us.

"Every emoti and its formation works in one exact frequency."

"That's the colours, right?"

Pedi nods. "All memories have frequencies too."

"And those are the colours of the shelves?" Manú asks.

"Similar colours are put together in seven different categories. The basic colour spectrum."

I look around. In one blue shelf area, several files are the wrong way round. Beside that it continues tidily and in violet. It's supposed to be seven. There's blue, but a bit lighter. Green, yellow, orange and we're standing right in front of a red shelf.

"What do the colours stand for?" I ask.

"That's not easy to understand. It's hard for me to explain. Somehow it has to do with how things are done energetically. The higher the frequency, the more energetic and light the emotis' actions can be. But this energeticness can be reduced because of overwhelming events."

"Did you get any of that?" I ask Manú. She shakes her head.

"Blue has a high frequency for example. Emotis in these colours can deal with complex situations phenomenally well." We continue on a few steps until we come to a pile on the floor. "The basic colours help me keep things in order," he says, as he picks up three files and puts them back into the blue shelf with a sigh. As he does this, a coffee cup is pushed out dangerously close to the edge.

"I saw one like that on that chaotic desk in the Office," Manú remembers in a whisper, while Pedi quickly tidies up a bit.

"So then you need blue shelves for blue files," I try to summarise.

Pedi laughs. "No, no. The frequencies do that themselves,

don't worry. I only have to check if any nonsense mixed colours appear. Then usually a file has been filed away wrong, one which doesn't fit into the frequency spectrum of the basic colour. Sometimes there are mistakes," he says, looking at the coffee cup on the shelf.

We continue on a bit. I'm fascinated by the diversity of the memories, the structure and, despite the exception, the order here.

"If I've understood correctly, then the information they assess in the Tower Office is compared with the memories in the files. How do the files get here?" asks Manú.

Pedi laughs. "Typical thinking from the world of things. Every piece of information has a specific frequency. So the categorisation and the connection to the files is already there."

"Does this categorisation come about when we identify something?" Pedi and I look at Manú, astonished.

"What do you mean 'identify'?" asks Pedi.

"I see something and recognise it's a shower mat," explains Manú.

"Yes. That's how it works," Pedi responds, almost enthusiastically. "And we call that labelling, when a new memory is created. The frequency for the new memory is kind of taken over from the frequency of the observation. Although, usually it's also influenced by other memories and also the intensification we talked about. So it's almost never a pure observation that gets recorded in the file."

"And what if there are already memories?"

"Then with something new, our attention is immediately connected to the memory and can be further processed in the Office. I'm sure Con explained that to you, right?"

"Yes, he did," I realise.

"And a shower mat memory like that belongs to the subject of cleaning the bathroom and bathroom accessories, or how should I imagine it?" asks Manú. She's figured out what he was getting at with the shower mat example. Now she's playing with my avoidance strategy, like a cat with a mouse. I feel very tired.

"Sometimes a pattern is created," explains Pedi perseveringly in the meantime. "A pattern contains several memories. A memory cluster like this is often intensified."

"Sounds complicated," Manú observes.

"All a question of routine," answers Pedi proudly. "In the example given, the mat is treated with special care. The pattern is then..."

"Isn't it all the ego that does things like that?" I ask in a flash. "It's all the ego, isn't it?"

Pedi looks surprised and thinks: "The ego, true, there was something. On the hill, the breakfast."

"At the Drachenberg?" I add eagerly.

Now Manú seems to be getting a bit nervous.

"You read something about yourself and what you call ego." He looks at Manú and then turns his gaze to me. "We think staying calm, having empathy and listening is the best approach." I should have known. This is getting personal. My stomach contracts or relaxes, I'm not sure which.

"You listened, that's all. That was our recommended strategy."

"I don't know if I'd talk about strategy in that case," I try to justify myself.

"Everything we do follows some strategy," says Pedi unmoved. What the hell is he saying?

"Then a few days later, the story," he continues, "in that case, it was about helping, doing something and showing that everything was alright."

Finally Manú asks a question to get us out of this sticky situation: "And so what or where is the ego?"

Pedi smiles to himself. "Do you really want to know?"

"Urgently," I blurt out.

"Patience, patience. One more thing first." He pauses for a moment.

"Do you think it was a coincidence that you had that dream where the Guardian appeared?"

"Wasn't it one?"

"The way you fixed your attention so intensely on the question about the ego – you wanted answers. Now you're here."

The last jump to a new subject was too big for me, but who cares. Now I'm dying to know what the deal is with the ego.

"You see," I say to Manú. "My time of worrying is over. Now we're going to get some answers."

"I don't get it."

"Then be careful you don't drop the penny before the penny drops."

"Go on."

"In the hut, in the forest. The kitchen with the garden hose."

"Yeah, showering behind the tree," remembers Manú.

"You told me about the ego there. That it feels strange that it should die. Ring a bell?"

"A quiet one," whispers Manú.

"You asked what would happen if the ego was gone and who would take over all its jobs then."

"You remember that?"

"I only asked that we leave the topic for another day, not that you forget it."

"You want me to click your like button now?"

Pedi seems to be amused too. Then he continues: "We didn't really know ourselves what Manú meant with the ego. That's why the Science Department got tasked with doing some more research."

"The Science Department? There's a UNIVERSITY here?" Manú can't hold herself back from laughing. "And what did they find out?"

"Fresh off the press." Pedi rummages around in some paper and then says: "There's no ego. Or there's none that calls itself that."

"No ego!" Manú's big eyes are waiting for more information.

"Ego, it's more…" he keeps searching. I've almost stopped breathing.

"…here it is. So, it's a principle – or maybe to put it better: our culture."

"The ego is your culture?" I repeat. "Then it's in every one of you, no matter what happens. It's always there?"

Manú's excitement is clearly taking a nosedive, if I'm reading her expression right.

"Yes, that's how it is. Ego is not a WHO, it's a HOW."

"So you can't get rid of it, nor can it be changed that easily," she concludes.

"Shame. I kind of hoped I had more influence. But then the ego can't die?"

"Die?" asks Pedi. "No, dying makes no sense. How ego culture develops also depends on the majority in the Parliament or the weather conditions, for example. Ask the Guardian, the detective or the Quiet One."

"So everything we're experiencing here began on the Drachenberg?" I conclude, after a brief pause to think.

"You got involved with this whole thing," Pedi nods.

"And if I don't want to be involved, what then?" I ask.

"Then usually new questions come up before there's time to deliver answers. It gets more and more hectic at the Office. Lots of file memories are reopened without understanding the links." Pedi shakes his head.

"Then it looks the way it does over there afterwards." He points to where the mess was in the blue shelf, which is still being watched over by a coffee cup.

We've now arrived at another part of the Archive. Pedi points at a sign: 'Pre-Birth'.

"Like in my ego story," I remember. "Then there must be 'Birth' too, which I guess is therefore 'The Beginning'?"

"The way you described it in the story."

"The only problem is," I admit, "I've never really understood what that meant."

Pedi ponders: "When the Archive was established, there must have already been files and memories. That was our only orientation for continuing our work."

"Where did these files come from?"

"I have no idea how that happened. I wasn't here back then. The Pre-Birth section..." he points to the shelves behind him, which almost seem transparent, "It has to do with ancestors. They're copies of their strongly intensified experiences. Life-threatening situations, dramatic memories especially are stored here. The colourless files are multi-frequencial. They're taken into account by an enormous number of enquiries."

"Did you understand that?" I ask Manú.

"So in other words, we have our parents' and grandparents' dramatic experiences in our system too – ancestral trauma, so to speak."

"Ancestral trauma is good." Pedi has to laugh, which makes him look a little less stern.

He wants us to follow him, we pass through several corridors. Doors open as if by magic. Hardly any light penetrates this part. It seems eerie and suddenly I'm finding it hard to breathe.

"These are the oldest files. No one normally goes down here. I heard from Miss Hildegard Intuition that some memories, like about the end, go back hundreds of generations."

"Everything feels so finite. It makes me think about death," says Manú quietly.

I shudder. Pedi looks in all directions. "Although some of us question it now and again, death is the end," he says finally.

I just can't make out the old files clearly. Pedi and Manú have already gone back. For a little while, I'm standing alone in this dark corner. Now it feels peaceful somehow. Quiet, like at the stones in the circle of trees. Strange.

In the meantime, Pedi has spread out some memories about the sports drama at school for us.

"Con told me that it's maybe not quite clear yet how things are linked in the files. Are you interested in hearing some details?"

Even before I can react somehow, Manú's kangaroo seems to have already pressed the 'yes' button. So I exhale the air again, which I had reserved for a we'd-love-to-but-we-really-should-be-going answer. I shrug my shoulders and accept defeat.

"Wonderful," says Pedi and points to the bottom experience in the file. I accept my fate, because Manú is about to find out another secret.

"You were standing on the gym equipment, a well-known situation actually – no reason to worry. But then something unexpected happened. The sweating, not having enough strength for the exercise, fear of failure. None of us were prepared for that. And then the humiliation in front of the whole class – that disgusted comment from that guy Kevin."

I cast a careful glance at the file. There it is, for real: "Ewww, gross." That's exactly what he said, in front of the whole class.

"Then the rejection, no one wanted to have anything to do with you, for a long time. That's why we increased the intensification of the memory bit by bit," Pedi explains and points to the three dots that are clearly marked on the file.

"The most successful strategy that developed after that was the rejection of any situations that seemed similar using sarcastic arguments. That has managed to avoid similar problems till now."

"Is that one of those patterns too?" asks Manú.

Pedi looks at me first, then Manú. "It is. Well recognised."

It seems they've decided for diplomacy in Manú's inner universe: "It's a possible solution that works again and again." Then she asks about alternative modes of action and Pedi turns the pages to the memory on top.

"Well, yes, recently something changed – a yoga session. We call that Y1 here. Despite our tried-and-tested recommendations, there was a new reaction, caused by you." He taps Manú's shoulder carefully.

"Normally once-off new experiences are no reason to put them in the file. But in this case a little bolt of lightning went through the system, which 'intensified' the new experience." Pedi looks at us expectantly. Apparently the next step is obvious.

"Y2 comes next?" Manú guesses.

"Not yet!" Pedi raises his finger. "Because of the intensification of the new experience, the file had to be changed.

So now the new experience is also activated as the first reaction. So the path was open to Y2, Y3 and so on."

We are sufficiently astonished and I wonder which of the many burning questions I can ask without completely outing myself.

"Why are the emotis so attached to the new experience all of a sudden? Couldn't they just ignore it and continue like before?"

"Usually they can. Only when new experiences are intensified or they were given a marker, then you get more energy for the new reaction than for the old."

"I heard all the words," I say then. "But understood?" My no-idea-what-you're-talking-about facial expression seems to work. Pedi looks at me. "You don't have to understand everything in two days. It's okay to have questions." Then he looks at Manú. "The Quiet One once said that to me. I always want to understand everything immediately.

"Open questions are like fertiliser for plants. They help them to grow so they bear fruit. And once there's fruit, the fertiliser is gone."

We look around a bit more in the Archive. The colourful shelf structure, files with experiences from other lives, the intensification of experiences, Pedi, to whom all of this seems completely normal. I also think I heard something about markets earlier. Whatever that means. My head is definitely spinning now.

On top of that: the ego doesn't exist. Who am I then, if all this is happening without my help? Why does Pedi have all this wonderfully in control and I don't even notice any of it?

Manú laughs and my thoughts are suddenly gone again. The tour of the Archive is over and Pedi leads us back to the entrance of the snail house.

"Finally!" exclaims the kangaroo, relieved. "This here is the Terrier." He points down.

We're greeted by an excited little dog, with brown and white patches, scurrying to and fro. Manú bends down and is immediately thoroughly inspected.

"Isn't this fascinating?" asks Manú.

"Fascinating? What do you mean?"

"Well how fast a little flash can change the files. And how long it takes until the markers make a difference."

"Yes, I think so. I mean, I…"

"…wasn't listening?" Manú finishes my sentence correctly.

"It's just a lot in one go." There's a buzzing in my head.

In the meantime, the Terrier is developing more and more affection for Manú. Then we arrive at our accommodation and our companions say goodbye.

"Pedi also said that these little flashes only happen rarely and most new experiences aren't even saved in the files."

"Oh really?"

"Especially when lots of experiences are happening at the same time or the weather is bad. Then the emotis just keep going as they did before, because it's easier to keep doing what's familiar."

"Stop." With a painful smile, I put up my hands: "Enough

of this flood of information. I kind of definitely want to know what you mean by 'the weather is bad'. But not today. I'm ready to hit the hay – I'm beat."

"Maybe we should stay a bit longer. It's so interesting, almost like magic." She looks at me expectantly. I'm too tired to say NO.

"One more thing," she raises her finger. "Before I forget, Pedi said we really should meet the detective."

"Meet the detective?"

"Yeah. That's all I know. Good night."

CHAPTER 10

Market Antics

At the market

After a very relaxing rest, we're now on our way to the Office. When we arrive, we see that the coffee-break area is packed. No surprise there.

Manú looks over at the bustling coffee drinkers, laughing: "I wonder how many markers they've added?"

"Did you understand that stuff with the markers yesterday?" I ask.

"Didn't you?" Manú narrows her eyes slightly. "I see, you were in stand-by mode again, were you?"

I try to come up with a smart answer.

"You know, if you don't answer for ten seconds it's a yes."

Smart answer. That's exactly the kind of thing I was looking for, but she got there first.

Then she says: "Markers also strengthen experiences."

"And where does a marker come from?"

"When something is repeated often enough, then

the new experience appears in the file and is taken into account?"

"How often does an experience need to be repeated then?" I ask full of hope about swift change in my life.

"Well, Pedi said usually around 40 times. It depends how different the new experience is from the previous procedures. The bigger the difference, the longer it takes until a marker is placed."

"So forty days of no cake and I'm rid of the problem," I say.

"No."

"What do you mean, no?"

"Because every new change requires more work and therefore means less energy. Old processes are familiar and easy. So less energy is required to implement the task."

"So despite the marker I can still break the new habit?"

"It's always possible," affirms Manú. "Old habits die hard."

"I've heard that thing with the forty times somewhere before," I remember. Was it Eric or my father?

"Jesus was in the desert for forty days," Manú offers.

"It wasn't him. It wasn't Buddha either."

"I guess we know them more from having breakfast and not from abstinence," Manú concurs.

"Hey, good morning to you."

Manú turns around and we are both facing the man all dressed in white. What was his name again? We find out that both Con and the kangaroo are not around today. So he suggests a spontaneous visit to the market. He says it's full of extraordinary, curious and amusing things.

Manú beams enthusiastically. I'm skeptical, but it seems the matter has already been decided. Full of motivation, our new tour guide strides ahead.

"Well then, have fun," someone says as they pass us, fully concentrated on trying to balance his coffee as he walks.

"I'm sorry, somehow your name has slipped my mind."

Our new tour guide looks at me: "That would be strange, because I never told you my name." A short laugh escapes his still closed mouth and makes a kind of grunting sound. Then he stands up poker-straight in front of us and offers Manú his hand with a distinct bow. And so we discover that Knightly White is usually known as the White Knight. Then I hear Manú say her full name for the first time: "Manú Sarah Kaytoni, it's a pleasure."

By now we've left the Tower and walked up a small path to the market. Suddenly an incredible hustle and bustle appears before us. Things are glittering and shining in every corner. The market seems unusually bright to me.

"It's not always like this," says the White Knight, "but the light forces are strong in the Parliament right now. Lovely, isn't it?"

"What do you mean by that?" I ask, confused. "Parliament?"

"I'll see if I can find the Politician, he knows the details. I'm sure he'll explain it to you."

It's no surprise that this doesn't even surprise me

anymore. So there's a politician too. Well luckily it's just one, however the Parliament works with just one politician.

"Wow!" Manú is really excited about all the action.

"What are they doing there?"

"They're playing Dramatica."

We look more closely. "How does that work?" asks Manú.

In a flash, the White Knight leaps over to the players. "Can we watch you play? These two don't know the game yet and they're dying to see it."

"A short explanation is enough for me," Manú says quietly. But the White Knight is already standing in the circle and we're close behind him. Grudgingly, the three players make space and deal new cards. One of them looks especially grumpily at the other players. He's dressed entirely in pink. He has a bag around his neck. While I'm still wondering what might be in there, the secret is revealed. A high-pitched bark gives away its content. The resident of the bag briefly pokes its head out – a quirky team.

The most popular game in the inner universe

"In Dramatica, you're playing for energy. Everyone places their bet, usually 10 quanta," the White Knight says to me quietly.

"I don't see any money," I say and ironically take a look under the table.

"Quanta, that's not-a currency."

"Aha," says Manú, "like the not-a wall?"

"No. It's a not-wall and not-a currency. The wall doesn't divide and yet keeps things out. With currency there's always automatically energy flowing when anything is done. Apart from that, the wall is visible and solid, the currency isn't."

"Visible, not visible?" I shake my head.

"Then 'not-energy' is energy that doesn't move?" asks Manú.

"Yes exactly, that's it: static, visible, 'not'. You identified that correctly, very good, really," the White Knight enthuses. Manú first looks at him and then at me. But the action of the game quickly grabs her attention again.

One player is resplendent in blue. In a highly dramatic way, he's telling the two others about the bad luck he had the day before. Another, in green, is listening to him with sympathy.

"The green guy is playing the saviour role," explains the White Knight. I look at him and laugh. "At some point, he'll try to take energy from the other guy with his wanting to help."

The slightly overweight, grumpy-seeming, pink-coloured guy with the handbag dog rolls his eyes and huffs.

"Do you see?" asks the White Knight. "The blue one is playing the victim. He's trying to work with the saviour to make it look like the third guy's fault. He must be to blame for the victim's misery. If he reacts like he's to blame, then the victim player will get energy from him."

"And the saviour?" asks Manú.

"He does sometimes too, depending on the situation."

"Aha," I say. Which basically means: I have no idea what you're talking about.

"The three characters: victim, saviour, persecutor, try to steal energy from each other."

"But I thought the victim and the saviour were working together?" asks Manú.

"They are. But still, the saviour is giving the victim and his invented problem attention. That's energy that the victim is getting from the saviour, even if they're working together."

"What's the point of playing something like that?" I ask.

"Because in the process we learn how we can steal energy from others."

"Others?" I ask.

"Well, other people, out there, in the world of form. That's where the principle gets applied."

"You mean, when we humans talk to each other, something exactly like that is happening?"

"Yes. Watch very carefully. You might recognise it in some conversations or arguments."

"But that's awful! And you just do it for fun?"

"It's part of our work – collecting energy, out there. Sure."

"The game starts with each player getting their role," continues the White Knight, completely unruffled. I look to Manú. At least she seems equally surprised. "This is insane!"

"And this insanity is happening in my inner universe?"

"Let's take the saviour. Every player pulls a card and puts it on the table," the White Knight continues without losing focus. "Whoever gets the highest intensity, so the highest number, can take on the role. If he doesn't want it, then the one with the second highest number can choose. If he doesn't want it, then the third person has to take it. The two others repeat the same thing for the victim role. Then the persecutor would automatically be the third person – which nobody wants to be of course."

"Because of their reputation?" I ask.

"Because of the low chance of getting energy. Usually the persecutor has to pay, especially if he's forced to act.

Manú thinks. "So if I say 'You never listen to me', then I'm the victim and you're the persecutor. Right?" She taps me unnecessarily as she says this.

"I do listen to you! What the hell?" I counter with fake outrage.

"That's exactly how it works," says the White Knight. "You react to the victim's story and pay for that with energy – because of the attention. Even anger is attention. The victim gets the quanta."

"Then I just need to not react too much."

"That would be perfect. Then the victim has to intensify his story, attack you, insult you. In that case, you'd get the attention, in other words, energy. Ah, if it were only that easy."

Slowly, I start to understand what's being played here and how these experts force me into the victim role again and again. I think of the bar situation with Manú after we played squash.

"Then usually the victim starts telling his story, which

then makes the person with the persecutor role an actual persecutor."

"I see," I say. "Now I'm curious to see what'll happen in the game.

"What about you?" I ask Manú, who has become audibly quiet. She widens her eyes and nods her head frantically, causing her hair to dance in all directions.

"I think they know that game in my inner universe too, I fear."

"All I'll say is zero percent alcohol," I whisper into her ear and in return I get a little shove.

"There are exceptions, but generally victims and saviours work together against the persecutor. If the persecutor reacts in a hostile manner, he pays in energy. If he doesn't react, then it gets interesting. Then the victim and the saviour have to come up with something."

"What might that be?" asks Manú.

"The victim could make the persecutor reactionless. The weather for example or institutions – you can't steal energy from them."

"That bunch up there do whatever they want anyway," I interject.

The White Knight nods. "Exactly! Then everyone's focus shifts to the saviour. Will he manage to manipulate the victim, or the other way round?"

The White Knight gives us each an approving pat on the back. I'm not sure if it's the game I don't like or the fact that I feel like I've been playing it for ages without knowing the rules.

"I'm still not entirely sure why the persecutor gets involved in the game at all. The others are always against him. Surely he has no chance of ever winning?"

Manú and the White Knight look at me. He shakes his head. "A persecutor can get control of the situation and then win. He could, for example, dominate the victim or make them look ridiculous."

I continue to watch the game. The player with the victim role falls silent. The saviour is talking to the victim non-stop and the persecutor is laughing gloatingly. Gradually the situation escalates. Suddenly one player pushes the table over. Startled, we jump to the side.

"Karpman," he shouts loudly into the circle. Then they gather up the cards and put the table back upright, nod and laugh.

"That was a clear win," says the green player, who had just been playing the saviour role. An assertive bark comes from inside the pink handbag.

"Who won?" asks Manú.

Since everyone at the table overheard this, the guy with the victim role says: "I did."

The others all agree.

The pink guy explains: "Complete attention. My ridicule and he just wouldn't shut up. Our friend here didn't react at all. All the energy went to him."

"What does 'Karpman' mean?" I ask.

"The end of the game. There's no victim, saviour, persecutor now. In the end, they're all stories they've told themselves."

"Is that the game's message?" asks Manú.

"Yes."

Curiosities at the market

We move on. "You must see this," asserts the White Knight and heads straight towards a stand, turns to us and gestures to one of the packets with both hands.

"Big trend right now – rental cookies."

I look at Manú, speechless. I'm getting more confused again, as Manú bursts out laughing and the man at the stand asks where the cookies are. When he is informed that she doesn't have any cookies, he shakes his head in astonishment.

Once again, the White Knight comes to the rescue and explains to us that you can give back rental cookies in exchange for a hearty smile.

"It's so popular here, nobody would think that you wouldn't know how rental cookies work."

"Did he really say rental cookies?" asks Manú.

"Three times, to be exact."

In the meantime, the White Knight tries to explain everything to the confused looking guy at the stand.

"That's how it is with tourists, you have to explain everything to them," I say to myself. I pick up one of these packets of cookies and take a closer look.

"And they have to touch everything," Manú adds.

"Very heavy for just cookies," I note.

"There was once a campaign about healthy eating," explains the White Knight, "and the question came up as to what it is that's so great about treats, because it's usually not the ingredients."

"And what was the result?" asks Manú.

"It's mainly the anticipation of enjoying such a treat that has the biggest effect."

"But when I eat the treat, that decreases – because of the satisfaction of the 'wanting to have'. The more I eat, the less enjoyment there is. In the end, it's basically been eaten up too."

"And all that happens without me noticing?"

"I guess that'll be different from now on," observes the White Knight. I shake my head. Manú's wide eyes suggest that it's also a new set of facts for her, these rental cookies.

"We started a little experiment, "the White Knight says. "Looking at the treats, imagining the perfect taste and enjoyment, but not eating anything. You could eat them, but you don't do it at first."

"Ha! Recently I tried to stop eating cake. There were at least two times when I was standing at the window of my favourite bakery, full of joy, imagining eating cake and cookies. I even dreamed about it. And every time, afterwards, my yearning for cheesecake and so on was gone."

"The result of this experiment was amazing," declares the White Knight. "It spread at lightning speed. Suddenly everyone wanted to try it and then someone came up with the idea of taking back these rental cookies. Now it's a total craze, especially at the market."

"How does it work? I mean you can't earn any money with it, can you? I buy myself cookies once and can look at them again and again?"

The White Knight looks at Manú smiling. "First of all, our currency isn't money. It's energy that I automatically get for actions, so for doing things. My motivation for having these cookies now determines the price, so the amount of energy that I will hand over for them."

"I see," says Manú.

"When you give back the cookies, twice the amount of energy gets exchanged: for the wanting-to-let-go and for the sincere-hearty-smile."

"Why would I want to give them back?" asks Manú.

"Yes; it's just built into it by the inventors. Because the rental cookies are really heavy."

"Now that's a business idea," I comment. "Very smart. Who came up with that?"

"The Science Department. They have so much fun inventing stuff."

"Crazy, sign me up right away," approves Manú.

"I think brilliant madness is a better way of putting it," I say and have already moved on to the next stand, where there are brightly coloured switches the size of dinner plates.

"Those are burp buttons. Want to try?"

While I decline, Manú has already pressed twice and is enjoying the result immensely.

"What do you need something like that for?" I ask.

"Pure pleasure," answers the salesman, smirking.

"And who's interested in them?"

"The ones from Section II; the Sports Area in Section III and also the ones from the party strip, they come by a lot," the seller informs me.

"We have one in the Office too," adds the White Knight. "But don't tell the Controlletti."

"Section II?" asks Manú.

"The Factory over there." He points to the large, brightly coloured building that we already noticed on our first tour with the kangaroo.

"Section II produces energy from the basic substances," the seller informs us. Then the White Knight adds: "You call that food. Stimulants and drugs are also processed there. Anything that can be eaten or drunk."

"And Section III is also the Factory?"

"Yes, exactly. All the other movements of energy and the energy management come together there."

"The drama game from before too?" I ask.

"Yes. That all gets coordinated in Section III."

We move on and the burp-button salesman says good-bye with a deep rolling burp, to which the squirrel in Manú answers with a high-pitched forced burp. I look away with slight embarrassment.

"What? It's all just energy anyway!"

What can I say to that?

Political understanding

"Hey, how are you?" The White Knight waves to another

visitor to the market, who then walks towards us. "May I introduce you? Preppy Politics, our politician, responsible for what goes on in the Parliament." Then another handshake. Shortly afterwards, Manú and I are standing with the politician at the drinks stand looking at three closed beer bottles.

"So they have more than just rental cookies here?" Manú realises.

"Is that really non-alcoholic?" I ask her, over-exaggerating. She then briefly rolls her eyes and examines her bottle in great detail. I have to laugh.

With two sentences, the White Knight has quickly tasked the politician with explaining the Parliament, then bids us farewell and heads back to the Office.

"Always ready, our White Knight," Preppy comments. We all watch him go. I think some of my friends already know this emoti and have totally unnecessarily criticised him as eccentric behaviour. Whatever.

The politician seems ready and willing to tell us everything about the Parliament, as has been decreed.

"In the Parliament, dear friends, the percentages are constantly shifting, emotis who put their frequencies in action more often create a greater intensity. In your terms, you could say they have more seats in the Parliament. Do you understand, dear listeners?"

Manú looks around. I too am not quite sure if the politician is only talking to us.

"Where do these majorities come from? I thought every emoti has only one frequency," I ask.

"A good question. I'll be happy to answer it."

Manú avoids eye contact, which is always a sign that she's about to burst out laughing. I'd definitely put a few quanta on the table for her thoughts, if that were possible.

"They're the basic colour spectrum. Seven of them. Each has a variation. Darker or lighter, but still yellow, for example."

"Like the shelves in the Archive?" Manú remembers.

"Absolutely correct. The basic colour spectrum helps orientation there."

"And what are the differences in colours then?" I ask.

"Higher frequencies – so energy vibrating higher – produce a bluish or violet basic colour and lower frequencies produce a reddish one."

Manú immediately asks: "Do higher frequencies mean more lightness, joy and flexibility in comparison to heaviness, frustration and laziness in the red area?"

The politician nods. "All requests that come into the Office, dear friends, are given a basic assessment. Do we happily accept the request or is there general rejection? That's what gets decided in the Parliament. Only then does the actual processing in the Office begin, leading ultimately to assigning the job to an emoti."

"So if I don't feel like doing yoga in the morning," Manú wonders, "then that's a majority of low frequency energy?"

"Red or orange," adds the politician.

"And so why do I do it anyway?"

"Then it's a slight majority. And the yoga Enthusiasts manage to get enough emotis on their side." The politician clasps his hands together and raises his arms. "We stand together, united!"

"Okaaaay."

"What's the current majority in the Parliament?" I ask.

"Sometimes it changes from situation to situation. But in the last few weeks, it's been a pretty stable blue-violet."

"Yes," I confirm, "I'm in a good mood, even get up early in the morning. Maybe it's because of the yoga?"

The politician shakes his head. "I have determined that the blue-violet majority in the Parliament has a direct link to the things you do together. You're in high spirits, my friends."

The laugh that was waiting to burst out of Manú finally liberates itself. The politician looks into the distance with a visionary expression and opens his arms wide. I see an expression on Manú's face that you might call "no words". I feel the heat rising inside me and would really like to just disappear right now.

Preppy turns his attention back to the audience. "Requests are more often positively assessed in this kind of majority situation," he adds.

"What are requests again?" Manú wants to know. These unfamiliar terms are confusing for me too.

Preppy thinks. "Usually requests come from outside – from the world of form. Seeing, hearing, tasting, smelling, touching – everything that is remarkable somehow and seems important is processed. The Office decides what that is. But there are also requests from emotis, who want to do things for their own benefit. That is not desirable, but it's widespread."

I shake my head. "How does that work? Seeing, hearing,

smelling probably aren't very important then, are they?"

"No, but thinking is. Some emotis try to force the Tower to activate them with fake requests to get more influence in the Parliament. They're powerful stories. Illusions that give the impression that they're important observations about the external world. And then they get processed in a completely normal way."

I have to laugh, although it's definitely not appropriate. "Sometimes I have the urgent need to just have a lazy day: pizza, cake, no movement, and pointless computer games and YouTube videos instead?"

"They are the typical effects of successful fake requests," the politician affirms. "Typical for the red-orange emotis."

"Why are these fake requests even accepted?"

"Sometimes just because of being constantly repeated. But mostly because of the convincing story."

I can hardly believe it. "Sabotage in your own system."

A short while later, the politician says goodbye to all his listeners and disappears. Suddenly we're standing alone in the market without a guide.

"What now?" I ask.

Manú looks around. "I'm interested in..." she starts.

Then suddenly, not far from us, I see a flat hat with a long feather dancing to and fro. I point over to it as the owner of this extravagant headwear waves at us. He ends his purchase with a friendly smile and comes towards us.

"Feel very welcome. On the heart line, here we meet. May no one be closed to the bustle of the market. Things trade themselves,

thoughts well formed. In everything, energy, so what trades itself in the end?"

"Oh hey!" answers Manú. This response doesn't exactly exhaust the potential of all possible responses. At least she appears a little startled.

"I'd like to thank you again for the helpful information you gave when we met. And now it's a bit clearer to me, how the ego works – culture." Was that a bit better?

The Guardian nods with a friendly smile. I notice how exhausting it can be to make high level, deep small talk. Do you call it deep talk then? Never mind.

"But we're still trying to understand exactly what the effects of this ego culture are."

The Guardian looks at both of us. No doubt Manú is relieved that I've brought up this subject and now nods with interest.

"A universe shows itself in details. The many things, all have a meaning. Yet what is more than the sum of itself? In the not-formed, there you will find. Can you understand the not-shown or understand the not-said? At the same time, you touch what encompasses all of our forms."

He tips his hat gently and bows. We follow suit, although a little more clumsily. And with that, he's gone.

"Well… I think…" Manú crosses her arms and taps her hand on her mouth. "He says that this world here reveals itself in all the many details and that that's how everything's connected. That's what I kind of understood anyway. But…" she shakes her head.

"It is very amusing to watch you think," I observe and hope to be overplaying my not-a-clue a little.

"I'm happy you find it so amusing," she says unaffected and immediately pulls me back to the issue of the Guardian's revelatory follow-up chat.

"What did he mean with that '...more than the sum of itself'?"

I shrug. I can't remember much more than snatches like 'not-said', 'not-formed' and 'not-shown'. Nonetheless, it seems to us, as he implied, that there's something bigger behind all this. And somewhere between all of it, we should be able to find the ego culture.

Who's talking there and why?

Our thoughts are interrupted, because my attention is drawn to three emotis talking excitedly. "Hey, maybe that's the detective?"

They're standing between two market stalls at a table. Looking from where we are, you might think they know each other well, maybe even are friends. They glance at one of the cookie packets in front of them.

We try to inconspicuously move close so we can hear the lively discussion.

One of them casts a glance in our direction. I instinctively duck behind a stall.

"You're not serious, are you?" Manú whispers to me, who's casually examining the wares displayed on a stall.

"What?"

"Acting inconspicuously means doing obvious things and NOT creeping around."

"I'm sure he didn't see me."

"Can you hear anything?" asks Manú.

"Only if you would shut up," I say. "Ouch!"

He looks in our direction again.

Then I hear: "More of the same..."

"Balance is destruction too. The weather has to change. Water is change, we have to get closer to the pure water."

"Will PR convince the others?"

"I hope so."

"We have to expect Free Radicals. We need arguments and counter-forces for that."

"Did you hear that too?" I ask Manú.

"Yes. I'm going over to the other side." And then she's gone and I keep listening to the conversation.

"Bushes are..."

"...lower the whole level."

It's hard to hear the third guy. He's standing right with his back to me.

Manú is back. "They're talking about bushes that are going to be planted and doing – I don't know – something else."

"Doing something else?" I repeat. "What does that mean?"

"I guess it's a metaphor. They want to get more from less..."

"You really are a very helpful detective, Miss Kaytoni."

"And then they were talking about the weather conditions and that they're lasting too long, which is threatening the balance and… then I came back."

"Aha, I see."

"A 'more of the same' will be produced, I also heard that. That makes sense, doesn't it?"

I look at Manú and have to laugh.

"Why are you laughing?" she asks.

"Your haul of information tells me that you've obviously also understood a lot of nothing."

"It has to do with the weather conditions. Pedi also mentioned that," she tries to convince me of the opposite.

"The weather conditions are supposed to change and with 'more of the same'? That doesn't sound very convincing."

"Shut up." She gives me a push.

"It was just a comparison," someone suddenly says behind us. "Dale Detective," the emoti introduces himself. "And yes, we were talking about the weather conditions. A very serious matter. Especially for tonight in the Creative Future Talk. Mr PR is going to talk about it there for the first time in public."

Weather conditions? What does that mean? Could you tell us more about that? These would have surely been adequate questions. But they stay stuck in my throat, despite my open mouth. Dale Detective laughs and kindly offers us a seat.

"I… how are… Apologies, we didn't want to disturb you, so…" Manú stops talking.

"Tom, nice to meet you," I say. Manú introduces herself

too. Then she manages to formulate a complete question. Dale Detective seems willing to fill us in. We sit facing each other. Him with his feet placed accurately alongside each other, his hands on his knees, with a friendly look on his face.

"There are underlying conditions here, which we describe as the weather. Like when there's fog, cold, warmth or wind where you come from. It influences everything."

"Might I imagine that," asks Manú, "like different moods?"

"Not exactly. The weather conditions have an influence on the prevailing mood. It's more like the result."

Manú thinks. "Then mood swings would be the result of April weather – something different every five minutes?" The detective laughs. "Maybe." He looks at Manú: "If you have a bit of a cold, then maybe you could compare it to damp weather."

"Hmm. How does that feel, having a cold?" she tries to imagine. To me the whole thing seems more like a fairy-tale, which Dale notices. "Are you still highly motivated then, ready for everything you need to do and unbelievably productive?" he asks me.

"No, of course not," I agree.

"What then? How does that feel for you, a cold like that?" Manú asks.

I close my eyes. A cold shiver goes through my body. Suddenly my nose feels tingly. And now it even starts to drizzle. "Bed is my safe island. I don't do much on days like that."

"The emotis' jobs don't get done," adds the detective. "What sense does it make to be active if they use up more energy for it than they get?"

"I see."

"However, it's still possible that the weather generates more attention, so feeds in more energy," the detective explains.

"How does that work?" I ask.

"When I was a student I broke my arm and had to walk around with a cast for weeks," Manú remembers. "So many people asked me about it. Friends helped me to cook, with my studies, even to get dressed. When it was over, I really missed being pampered."

"So the weather conditions always depend on external circumstances?" I conclude.

"Yes, external factors are always involved, which lead to specific weather conditions," Dale confirms to me. Manú's example with her arm goes through my mind. Then I see the link to our subject matter. "And? What kind of weather conditions were they?"

"Afterwards my arm was so thin and so unfit, I'd say it was a long period of drought."

"That's a good one," I have to laugh. "Does the example fit?" I ask the detective.

Yes, definitely. And if you did sports after that and you felt good, but maybe a bit tired, then that would also have an influence on the weather."

"Now I'm slowly starting to understand why they're called weather conditions," I say. "Work while it's raining, it's possible. But then everything gets wet and cold, and I have to deal with that as well."

"We're currently seeing heat and dryness," says the detective with a concerned look. "That tipped the Garden Fields off balance. All those bushes are drying out."

"Why are there so many of them?"

"Someone, who they call the Glutton around here, started planting them all over his Garden Field. Supposedly, they don't need any care and still provide the vital energy desired."

"I'm guessing there's going to be a 'but'," I add.

"Absolutely, there is a BUT. The Science Department studied it and found out that vital energy is produced, but only at a very low intensity. It doesn't strengthen the self-healing capacity of each emoti. A shock."

"I don't understand. It's only a problem with one Garden Field and not all of them. Right?"

"Well, by now lots of other emotis planted the same bushes. There are lots of them, but they don't produce much. But the garden system is trying to balance this out. So the yield in all the Garden Fields is lower."

"Oh dear."

"At first no one really noticed. But now, with the dryness and heat, the bushes can't take it without being cared for. No one's looking after them and so they turn into these thorny, dry bushes. They don't provide anything anymore and are lowering the overall vital energy in the Garden Fields dramatically."

The detective stands up. "I recommend that you come to the Creative Future Talk tonight. Then you can find out more about our problem."

He looks at us expectantly. I nod. Every corner of Manú's face is already shining with a yes.

"Where will this Creative Future Talk take place?" I ask.

"In the Tower Office."

"Not far, great," says Manú. Then we say goodbye to Dale Detective, certainly a bit odd, but definitely very likeable.

Back at our accommodation, it's time for a power nap again, which I hope is going to give me the energy for the Creative Future talk that evening. I've arranged to meet Manú in the Tower Office, where Mr PR will explain the problems with the weather conditions and the dry bushes in public. Is this expanding my consciousness, learning all this stuff here? I wonder and then immediately fall into a deep sleep.

CHAPTER 11

Creative Future Talk

Creative Future Talk – today: Mr PR live on stage

Once I'm awake again, the first thing I think is that I need to prepare for the Creative Future Talk. Well, really all that means is that I feel a bit strange, because I'm going there on my own. I have no idea if I'll find Manú when I get there. I climb the stairs at a leisurely pace and see Mr PR through a half-open door. He's leafing through some bright blue coloured papers, pacing up and down. Then he notices me, nods briefly and disappears from the crack in the door. I continue and enter the Office, which has been completely cleared of the usual furniture.

The now empty room, which seems brighter than yesterday, fills up quickly. Some people nearby notice me looking uncertainly at the little stage in the middle of the room and one of them says: "In the Creative Future Talks the speakers always stand in the middle of the room surrounded by the people listening." I ask and they tell me Mr PR is a big hit and can really electrify the audience. The crowd bursts into applause when he steps onto the small stage.

"Do you remember what it's like when all the gardens are blooming? The air filled with fragrance."

The room falls silent. I look for Manú in the crowd.

"That is love, that is our life."

Everyone's attention is totally focussed on the middle of the room, on this one single figure, who is once again wearing a bright, colourful suit. He has a pink folded handkerchief in the breast pocket. When he turns around to speak to the listeners on the other side, his long hair sweeps around with him.

"The Garden Fields. They're in danger, more than ever before. More and more of the bushes are drying out. That's our tragic reality. Weak, dry bushes, uselessly turning countless garden fields into barren land. We need diversity again. We need all the plants, which are an expression for the many types of soil in which they grow. We will lose our vitality, dear friends, if we don't bring back that diversity."

Silence again. A murmur goes through the crowd. But what does he mean by 'vitality'? I look to the stage, because Mr PR is holding something up in the air. The blue pieces of paper from before.

"What is written here proves it! A report on our investigation. Where is the problem coming from, we asked ourselves: in cooperation with the Science Department and my humble self, the reputable Dale Detective went in search of the causes and connections. And we're shocked. There's no doubt, dear friends. The trail leads to the Factory, to Section II of the Factory. The trail leads…" Mr PR suddenly lowers his voice, "…to Ben."

Who's Ben? It's so quiet you could hear a pin drop.

"This is especially hard for me to hear. But this is about all of our welfare. And yes, he's my brother, but he's the key to all the problems here."

Did I just hear him say brother?

"I'm afraid I have to inform you," his voice takes on an ominous tone, "that Section II of our Factory got out of control."

Another murmur followed by lively mumbling spreads through the rows.

"We must act," which is greeted with loud cheers of support. One voice shouts: "But how? What can we do?"

I spot Manú very close to the guy shouting. Now and again, she says something to someone I've never seen before.

"There is a link to the Free Radicals, dear friends. Supposedly, with the bushes, they found something that could bring them their vital energy without any affection and care from the Garden Fields. Then everyone planted these bushes and that's what tipped the garden's ecosystem off balance. The intensity of all of our vital energy has dropped. And it's continuing to drop, because these supposed miracle bushes are drying out and aren't providing anything at all anymore."

"What does that have to do with us?" someone shouts from the crowd. "It's their problem."

"We need diversity in the system, otherwise every single one of us is done for. It's tough for me to say this, but my brother is now abusing the basic substances from Section II to create a replacement."

"A replacement for what?"

Mr PR searches for the right words. The room falls silent again. He looks out at the crowd of listeners, to the left and then to the right, then takes a deep breath. "We suspected what might be behind all this. Now we know for sure. The Free Radicals are meeting more and more often for their orgies of eating and drinking. It seems that they get what they lost in the Garden Fields there. And it's been going on for a long time, without us noticing. Only it's never been as out of control as it is now. That's all in here too." Once again he holds up the report.

"We all know that the quality of the basic substances has deteriorated. But only now do we know why. Demand change! Get back the vital power of your Garden Fields! And support us to save Section II. Because right now it's on its way to ruin."

I'm getting hot. I think many of the others are also slowly starting to understand the gravity of the situation.

"How are we supposed to start doing that?" someone shouts from the crowd again. The agitation in the crowd is followed by a slight sense of panic.

"Don't ignore it. Talk about it, everywhere. We all have to know what's going on. That makes them nervous. That'll drag them out of their hiding places."

A bit of applause mixes with mumbling that is now getting louder.

"We know about the junk in the Factory and beyond. You must have noticed it too." PR's voice drowns out the audience. Everyone looks back to the stage.

"Rubbish is spreading all over the place. Where do you think this junk comes from? It is made of the absolute worst basic substances, which are harmful for us all. Lots of it and cheap. That's all they care about in the Factory now – lots and cheap," he repeats slowly for emphasis.

"Sometimes the quality of the basic substances is so bad that we might as well already call it junk, before it's even transformed into something else." Once again Mr PR holds up the report. The applause and cheering get louder. After the initial shock, more and more of them seem prepared to do what Mr PR is asking.

Basic substances, junk, orgies, Section II. I think of my last food binge. What's me, what's not me? It's hot here. I need to sit down.

"No one is taking care of the bushes in the Garden Fields anymore. They're drying out and making the vital energy disappear. Your Garden Fields! Your vital energy! The bad basic substances have caused the heat and dryness."

Is that why I'm always sweating, I wonder? Is that the heat that keeps coming over me? Do the basic substances have so much influence on everything?

Shrill cries tear me away from my thoughts. "Conspiracy! You're just dragging your private feud out in public.

Do it better! But you don't know how. That's what's going on. You can't do it!" someone shouts not far from me.

I get up out of my chair. Who was that?

Mr PR counters: "Dear friends, recognise the danger. You're going to ruin us all if you buy those cheap thrills."

There are boos all around me. The mood is getting more heated. The crowd's attention shifts towards me. "You're a plague," someone shouts in my direction.

"We'll stop you."

"We want to know what you're up to."

More and more emotis join in. I look for Manú again, but I can't see her anywhere. Who are they? What's going on here? The cries get louder and louder, but I can't understand what they're saying anymore. I have to get out of here. Where's the exit? Outside, I take a deep breath and look for another way back into the action. But I can't find one, so I just retreat.

Surprise – after a heated debate

When I get to my room, Manú is already waiting for me. "So, what do you say?" She smiles at me. She knows something.

"Pretty heated atmosphere. Fits the issue."

She nods.

"Go on, tell me. What happened with you?"

"Do you know what FR means?"

I shrug.

"The Free Radicals. They're supposed to be misusing basic substances from the Factory to make a kind of drug energy. It does relax you, but also makes you a bit slow. The Gourmet refers to that ironically as a food coma."

"Who?"

"I just met him. He works in Section II too and knows what's going on there pretty exactly. He was the one who convinced Mr PR to hold the talk. And he got Dale Detective access to Section II."

"What are these basic substances?" I ask after a pause for thought.

"Anything to do with eating and drinking are the basic substances here. Someone already told us about them. Remember?"

Clearly I don't.

"Sounds interesting. And this strange guy…"

"Gourmet. The Gourmet, he's a really nice emoti."

"And he just volunteered all this information?"

Manú nods with approval.

"Very interesting."

"Great. Then I'm sure you'll be happy to know that the Gourmet has invited us to Section II. I said we'd come," she announces, looking at me expectantly.

"You did what?"

"We're going there in the morning, to the Factory!"

I can't come up with anything to counter this determination today. A yawn announces the end of our little post-creative-future-talk talk. "Then we're going to Section II tomorrow I guess. What else?" I ask weakly.

Manú doesn't hear the sarcastic undertone. She seems content with how the evening went and goes into her room.

Later, in bed, the same question keeps running through my head: Why did Manú just decide we'd go like that? She can't just...

I get up. Her room seems completely quiet. So I go back to bed, listen to myself breathing. Turn to the left, then to the right.

Suddenly, in one jump, I'm standing beside my bed. What? Where? Then I hear a voice. Manú is cautiously coming towards me and sits down on the edge of the bed.

"Were you dreaming?" she asks quietly.

"Why didn't you just ask me?" The words stumble out of me before I can form a clear thought.

"How? I couldn't find you anywhere."

"Well then you should wait before you agree to things like that, damn it!"

Manú pulls back a little, startled. She stands up.

"Why does anything about the Factory make you so angry? We looked at the other places together too. It's probably really interesting."

"It's my business how I deal with it," I burst out. Manú doesn't reply.

Her silence gets on my nerves.

"You just have to ask. Is that so hard?"

"Ask, ask! My God, I just didn't think of it. Anyway I was surprised when he invited me too. You're acting like I embarrassed you in public. What's the problem anyway?"

Manú's face is flushed. I've never seen her so angry and so loud.

"Now you want me to…"

"No! But maybe you can stop acting like you're so unbelievably important!" Manú shouts. "Oh, someone did something awful to you. Someone dared to make a mistake."

She opens the door and leaves. Before I can stop her, she's gone.

I throw myself onto the bed. What seems like a moment later, there's a knock. The kangaroo and the Terrier are waiting to bring us to the Factory. Did they just hear everything?

"I'm coming." A chair falls over. Then I stumble across the room. I just want to leave. But how? Is it even possible?

"Are you coming?"

"Yes!"

CHAPTER 12

Something in the Air

Bad atmosphere

We walk past the market and some other structures in silence. Again I notice the dry bushes all over the place in the yellowish grey of the Garden Fields. There's lots of activity in the other parts of the gardens, but there's no one at all near the bushes.

Once we arrive at the Factory, the kangaroo points at an area in the middle. The Terrier trots on ahead and jumps up at a large gate several times. Looks like that's the way in. With an unusually serious voice, the kangaroo tells us: "We'll pick you up again from here later. Just wait."

Then both of them disappear. The heavy gate opens with loud creaking sounds. I take a deep breath. I catch a glimpse of a certain look on Manú's face from the corner of my eye. Has she been crying? That very moment, a fit-looking, energetic emoti comes towards us at a brisk pace.

"Welcome to Section II of our Factory. Everything that can be eaten or drunk passes through our Factory floors."

Manú nods at him and smiles. The two of them start casually chatting. I feel like a third wheel. His warmth and friendliness are the total opposite of my mood right now. On top of that, it seems like Manú is trying to make me feel like she's completely fine and doesn't need me for this. This thought makes me even more annoyed. I barely listen to half of what the Gourmet enthusiastically has to say. Of course Manú is hanging on his every word.

Suddenly someone calls over to us in a squeaky but loud drawl.

"Did we discuss you being allowed to spread your fairy stories here?"

Before I can properly see who this unpleasant voice belongs to, the door closes and for a moment it's quiet. Suddenly I'm fully present. My eyes meet Manú's. We both shrug our shoulders simultaneously.

The Gourmet flashes an artificial smile. "I guess that was our boss," he says, trying to downplay the situation.

"I don't usually talk badly of people, but he's just a constant challenge. And always with that stupid handbag dog at his chest, it looks ridiculous."

"Then we know him from the Market," Manú realises.

"What?" the Gourmet asks.

"Those three emotis who were playing that Dramatica game. He was one of them."

I nod. "I definitely remember the handbag dog."

"The Tiger almost ate the dog once. Ever since, he only peeks out of that pink handbag and starts barking at the worst possible moments," the Gourmet explains.

"And who's the guy carrying around this dog in a handbag?" I ask.

"That's the Glutton," the Gourmet answers quietly. "He's the one causing all the problems. That was why we held the meeting yesterday."

"He's the guy with the bushes, the junk and the heatwave it's causing?" I ask.

The Gourmet nods and now looks even more concerned.

"The inspiration of food, freshness, flavour, aroma and the energy you gain from it, that's my passion. That's my life. Experiencing a symphony of flavour with every bite of fine food. For me it's meditation and pure joy of life at the same time."

"Wow!" Manú seems bowled over.

"And what's the Glutton about?" I ask cautiously.

"He has no idea about that stuff. Tough words, loud and vulgar, as you just saw. That's what we live with every day now."

We don't say anything for a moment. I have a lump in my throat. I have a cramp in my stomach too. Why have I never noticed the Gourmet before? It's always the Glutton I experience while eating. At least that's what it seems like when I see all this.

"It's so simple: eat less, but better quality ingredients. Fresh basic substances just have the best quality. It's so easy and so enjoyable too."

"Basic substances?" I ask. Somehow I keep getting confused about this term.

"Everything that comes in here. Everything that's been eaten or drunk, those are the basic substances. They go on to make all the energy that's available as basic energy in the inner universe. We also supply the Garden Fields – with catalyst substances, because they accelerate growth. But the kinds of basic substances we're processing at the moment are growing nothing but dry bushes and are causing a drought in the whole system."

"What do you do with the plants anyway?" I ask.

"They transform every form of energy into the type of energy that the emoti who's looking after the garden field where they're growing needs. It's a huge help to the low vibrating emotis especially. In that way, they can carry out their work properly and don't have to hustle for energy on the sly."

Slowly, I'm starting to realise why the thorny bushes gave me the creeps on our tour at the start. It's all connected to the problem that's being caused by this gluttonous emoti. No wonder I felt so much resistance about coming here with Manú. It had nothing to do with her. I smile at her. She looks back, still rather skeptically.

"If only the others would just listen to me a bit," the Gourmet says, more to himself.

"How many emotis work in Section II?" asks Manú.

"If you count the handbag dog, whose name is Pinkie by the way, then there are five of us."

"Do we know the others already? I mean, have we met them?" I ask, mainly myself, after all the Gourmet isn't a mind reader.

"The Glutton, Pinkie, the Tiger, the Cake King and me. My ideas about our work here are the opposite to what all the others think."

I nod. "What does a tiger do in a Factory?" I ask.

"At the moment, he finds the basic substances the Glutton uses for his feeding frenzies. He creeps around Section II. Turns up unexpectedly all over the place and sniffs around."

Manú doesn't ask any questions, which I'm sure she normally would. Our stupid fight. My attempts to try to catch her eye fail. I'd like to give her a sign that I'm sorry. She doesn't notice. Deliberately? Is she trying to let me know that I did something wrong? I'm such an idiot for accusing her of all those things. Is it over between us? Who would want to hang around with a guy like me?

"Oh God!" exclaims Manú, which immediately sweeps away my thoughts. "It's so awful how this Glutton is running this place!" she affirms, sure that I have heard everything the Gourmet just said.

"Can't anything be done?" I ask, hoping to quickly grasp what they're talking about. Silence.

"Plenty, cheap and secret, that's how they work with basic substances here. A lot of junk is created. The Factory is going to the dogs. Some emotis don't have enough energy to develop properly."

"What do you mean by that?" Manú asks.

"They can't develop any joy, vitality, lightness. How can yoga be fun if there are too many basic substances in the way everywhere?" the Gourmet asks without really expecting an answer. This hits me hard.

We all jump slightly as we suddenly realise the Glutton is marching towards us with the Tiger. Both of them look very angry.

"Who asked you and who allowed you to spread your nonsense? Get out of here!"

"We asked and we want to know," Manú says with determination.

The Glutton pays no attention to her, but steps closer to the Gourmet. "Get out of here," he repeats, fuming.

The Gourmet takes a step back, gives us a quick nod and is about to go.

Then suddenly I'm gripped by a rage I've never experienced before.

"Stop!" I shout at the Glutton and step so close to him that you could barely fit a sheet of paper between us. "You're terrorising my inner world!" I scream, completely losing it. The Tiger shrinks back, startled, and seems ready to run.

"Why?" echoes through the Factory floors.

"How dare you shout at the Gourmet? And why are you ignoring Manú? I'll rip you to shreds!" My voice cracks with anger. I'm ready for anything, which the Glutton seems to understand, since he takes two steps back and raises his hands in a conciliatory gesture.

"Calm down, calm down. What's got your panties in such a twist?" Pinkie has retreated fully into his handbag.

"Who do you think you are? What a complete idiot!

You act like the boss, but you have no idea what needs to be done here." I hit the handbag hard with my hand by accident. Pinkie lets out a yelp and the Glutton turns away to protect him.

"You will get out of here immediately," I scream. "And we're going to continue our tour with the Gourmet. You should be fired immediately!"

Now the Glutton tries to talk me round, even subserviently apologises to the Gourmet, which only makes me even angrier. I inhale loudly and walk towards him again. He runs towards the door and slams it behind him. The Tiger is long gone. I take a deep breath in and out. Then I look straight at Manú and the Gourmet.

"I feel better now. It's my inner universe anyway. If I have to put up with all this madness then at least I get to decide what happens here."

It's quieter now, or rather silent, you could hear a snowflake fall. I slowly realise what I've done. As do the others.

"Thank you," says the Gourmet. He looks at me, beaming. We all feel his relief.

"If only I had known." I stop. Yeah, what then?

Now the Gourmet put his heart and soul into showing us how to transform the right basic substances into energy. He tells us what qualities the basic substances need to have so that this process isn't extra work for Section II. He explains that extra work due to bad basic substances always means more energy is required for the processing. Sometimes it's even so bad that more energy is consumed than produced. He shows us the dumps full of junk that have been created as a result of processing bad basic substances. I'm shocked.

It feels like a war, like a battlefield, that has spread throughout the Factory. And the warmonger is the Glutton, along with his followers. How can the Gourmet even survive? The joy he feels when wonderful basic substances are transformed is being completely suffocated in this awful Factory. My eyes fill with tears. I turn to the side and quickly wipe them away.

Back in my sleeping quarters, I don't know what to do with myself. From the bed to the window to the chair, then back to bed. I curl up into a ball on the big duvet. A deep sadness washes over me and with it, the tears reappear. I can't remember the last time I felt so awful.

Slowly, the door opens and someone carefully puts a hand on my shoulder. I hate Manú seeing me like this. But her hand on my shoulder feels good.

"Ca...n we do a... che...ck-in?"

She nods. "Sure, let's talk."

So I start: "I want to le...ave here, just go. But ru... running away..."

I take a deep breath.

"...It's not an option for me anymore. Running away from myself, I know that too well and I've do...ne it so many times before. I'm here now, I'm going to stay. Now I'm going to look, take a very close look. I want to know what's going on here... And I'm really sorry about our fight. I'm sorry. Thanks for listening."

PART III

WHEN THINGS CHANGE – FOR GOOD?

CHAPTER 13

Manú in the Reflection of the Lake

The next morning

The next morning, there's a quiet knock on the door. I jump out of bed. Where am I? Manú enters cautiously.

"You won't believe the dream I had," I say. "I was with you in my inner universe and I fired this guy there. Totally crazy."

Manú looks at me, eyes wide. She laughs. "I know. I was there."

I look around confused. "So only totally crazy?"

Diplomatically, she doesn't reply and sits down in lotus. She looks at me, longer than usual.

"I still owe you an answer."

"Really?"

"Yesterday, after the check-in, I remembered."

"Give me a minute to freshen up."

A few minutes later I'm sitting on my cushion facing her.

She looks at the floor. We say nothing for quite a while. Then, suddenly: "I just wasn't there."

"What do you mean?"

"It was a lovely day. My friends and I, outside on my favourite meadow beside the woods. We were playing hide and seek when my father came walking across the field."

I have to swallow audibly.

"He called out for me hoarsely. I left my hiding place hesitantly. He took me in his arms silently. 'Your grandmother has died,' is all he said."

I feel a sudden shock. I want to say something, but my voice doesn't seem to work.

"I tore myself free. 'No!' I screamed. 'Never!' He held me tight. It was the first time I ever saw him cry."

"What happened?" I ask quietly.

"She was hit by a car when she was on her way to visit my grandfather's grave. The last thing she said was: 'Where's my Manú?'"

I try to overcome the inertia of my shock and put my hand on her shoulder.

"I wasn't there, do you understand?"

I move closer and stroke her back. I should breathe if I want to say something.

"Do you feel guilty, because you couldn't be there?"

"I used to. Now I know that there's nothing I could have done. Still, I always get nervous when someone's late or doesn't turn up and I don't know why."

"You can't just forget about experiences like that, just because your head says it's not your fault," I say.

"It was a problem in my last relationship. He was always late. Changed plans at the last minute, and didn't think it was important to inform me."

I know that feeling, I suddenly realise. "You're standing there, waiting and waiting, and no one comes," I say quietly, "And you don't know what you should do."

"I get totally overcome by this unbelievable helplessness, almost panic," she says.

I feel kind of awkward doing it, but I put my arms around her. She puts her head on my chest.

"How old were you?" I ask.

"Ten."

It's quiet. Then I feel her sobbing rhythmically against my chest.

"She was my best friend, my rock. She was always there for me. Then she was gone, just like that."

"Unimaginable." I take a deep breath.

"Three months later, we moved house. Then all my friends were gone too."

"Why did you move?"

"It was her house – and my parents didn't want to keep it. Don't know why. I'm not interested either. I couldn't care less about my weird relations!"

"Did you move far away?"

"267 km. Rathenow. And then to Weimar."

"That's not that far."

"At ten, it's like the other side of the world."

"I understand."

"At the cabin you asked me where I had experienced God."

I frown. "Oh! True. And you postponed the subject."

"At home, there's this lake. After she died I sat there nearly every day – for hours. Then one day I saw her."

"How do you mean?"

"In the reflection of the lake. She spoke to me, just like that."

I nod.

"We talked often at the lake, for weeks. One day she said: 'I have to go now. You take care of yourself – promise?' I promised her."

Manú falls silent.

"You carry her in your heart."

"That was two weeks before we moved away."

A shiver runs down my spine.

"Ever since then I know that God exists. Whatever that might look like. He's just there. Usually without saying much. Sometimes he's talkative – if we listen. If we really listen."

"And you really listened at the lake."

She nods; my hand is still resting on her back. We just sit there like that. Suddenly I like the silence. More and more familiar, it feels very natural now.

CHAPTER 14

Let's Have a Word, or Two

When things become

After a visit to the Market, I'm now on my way to the Office. Manú is taking a little time for herself. She wanted to be alone. I saw her last at the wall not far from the entrance gate. The Guardian gave her a nod.

When I've gone upstairs, I'm welcomed by the detective. Has he been waiting for me?

"Good to see you. Let's go over here. Please follow me. I have to talk to you."

I follow him. We take a seat.

Dale looks at me. "I saw you last night."

"Yeah, was a very interesting evening."

Dale nods. "Am I correct in assuming that you didn't understand everything?"

Hesitantly, I confirm his assumption.

"It's important that you understand."

"Why?"

"Let me explain. If that's okay for you?"

"Why was there all that hostility towards Mr PR? Why was the whole thing so heated?"

"The opponents who were there belong to the Free Radicals, a group that sees a conspiracy in everything."

"Conspiracy?"

"Yes. For example they think the birth date is being misused."

I have to laugh. "What the hell?"

"It's about personal freedom for them."

"That's not necessarily a bad thing," I remark.

"Exactly, not necessarily. The problem with conspiracies is that they don't take the complexity of many entities living together into account. Usually they think it's a handful of evil individuals, steering and controlling everything. They don't want to understand that there are systemic problems, which certain individuals always have a big opinion on, but could never get under control entirely."

I think about it and am amazed at the far-sighted and wise things that go on inside me without me really realising.

"But in the end, there are always problems," Dale adds, "because the Free Radicals do things in a very extreme and radical way."

"Doesn't behaviour like that get attention and therefore energy?"

"Exactly right. I see you understand what's going on here."

I nod. Some things are in fact becoming clear to me.

"But the Free Radicals also like to party that way. They use the basic substances from the Factory in unbelievably huge amounts for these, these…"

The detective looks disgusted: "Eating orgies."

I have to swallow.

"The consequences are huge. The dry bushes. They're all over the Garden Fields."

"What does that have to do with it?"

"Well, a certain amount of vital energy always comes out of the basic substances, just like out of the plants in the Garden Fields. Because the bushes are drying out, they're not providing anything anymore. So now the Free Radicals think if they consume enough basic substances, it'll be enough. But they forget about quality. There's nothing in cheap basic substances."

"Why cheap basic substances?"

"Cheap is one of the main principles of the Glutton – Ben Relations. He has control of all the basic substances."

"The Glutton's real name is Relations?" I ask with amazement.

"Yes, he's Paul's brother, who's now called Public Relations."

"True. And still, totally mad. And he's one of the Free Radicals too, this Ben?"

"He's the chairman. He's the fulcrum of the problem. He rules over Section II and therefore controls the basic substances."

"So he and the Free Radicals are linked to the eating problems I've been struggling with forever?"

"It's a kind of drug energy, which is transformed from the permanent surplus of basic substances," adds Dale. "That's why these feeding frenzies keep happening. They get themselves into a state of gluttonous fullness – that's the drug it seems."

Trouble at the Factory

"And what does that have to do with the weather conditions?" I ask.

"A big portion of the basic energy for the whole inner universe comes from Section II. It's available to everyone. The character of this energy is very important in determining the weather conditions. The weak energy, which we have a surplus of now, causes the dryness."

I nod, even though I still don't totally get it. Dale places his feet exactly parallel to each other. "No one knows why it all happened. One day Ben Relations turned up in the Factory and just took over."

"You mean he doesn't actually belong there?"

Dale nods emphatically. "He was actually pure joy, providing the most wonderful surprises. Then he was gone for a long time and one day he just turned up in Section II."

"So why does everyone call him the Glutton?"

"The piles of junk, his angry attitude, his whole appearance suggests gluttony."

I consider for a moment, look over to the Factory. "How was that possible? Somebody must have let him in?"

"In the beginning, he just helped out. He was interested, dedicated, helpful. But soon the Gourmet had been pushed aside. Ben just ignored him. The Gourmet wasn't strong enough to stand up to him."

I take a deep breath. "When was that?"

Dale ponders. "It must be 22 years ago now."

I calculate quickly. "The gym class?" What else happened around that time? I can remember fragments. The high bar, wet with sweat. The laughing. I hear it ringing in my ears all over again. And then? What happened then?

"In the beginning, no one noticed what was happening in Section II. For a long time, the Gourmet didn't say anything about it. I only found out more recently. Actually, the Gourmet and Mr PR asked me to investigate the situation. What's coming out is shocking. And when the link to the Garden Fields became clear, it really scared all of us."

Dale leans over slightly towards me. "Your meeting with the Glutton yesterday gave us all a lot of hope. I'm convinced only you can solve the problem. We just can't compete with the power of Ben Relations and the Free Radicals. You have to make sure he loses his power. Make the Gourmet strong again, back in charge of Section II."

"Me? Why me? I don't know. What can be done? I don't even know..."

"You have to help to straighten things out. Help the inner universe. Help yourself."

"You're wrong. I'm sorry, but I can't do it, I know I can't."

The detective says nothing, looks down at the floor. He

nods gently, which calms me down, because it seems to mean he accepts what I'm saying.

"I'd like to introduce you to someone," he says finally.

The detective stands up. "Come with me."

What's he planning to do? We leave the Tower and head towards the Garden Fields.

"Ben Relations isn't going to just disappear from Section II," he begins to say in passing as we walk.

"Actually I think the Gourmet is going to suffer even more now. The Glutton must know now who was behind what happened, your meeting him, the Creative Future Talk and all this information being spread."

"Oh no!" I stop in my tracks. "But that shows how little I can do. The opposite, I'm just making things worse."

"The Gourmet needs help. He needs you. Please, this way."

Reluctantly, I continue walking. No, it's not my business to be fighting against the Glutton. I can't do it. No way.

A garden is...

We go to the Garden Fields. A very special figure emerges from a sweet-smelling labyrinth. A veil a bit like a dress flows gently around her elegant shape. A bright yellow can be seen in the mist that seems to almost dance around her.

"Miss Intuition." Dale takes a slightly longer bow.

Miss? Intuition? The yin-yang symbol pops into my head. Dale turns to me. "Miss Hildegard Intuition, the guardian of the gardens."

"Welcome, familiar newcomer." She smiles. "Let's go." She gestures to the white roses that are entwined around the entrance to the labyrinth and allows me to walk ahead.

"A garden is your love," she says suddenly. "In the garden, you're closest to God."

"What do you mean by that?" I ask, astonished.

"Birth, death, the seasons of the year, the gifts from Mother Earth and all the different wonders of her insignificant and great beauty. Here's a fragrance sweet as roses, here's one as gentle as apples."

Two squirrels are chasing each other among the flowers, without crushing them. What are they doing here, I ask myself silently.

"They represent your vitality, your flexibility, your lightness."

I watch the two as they go. They stop for a moment, stand up on their hindlegs, look at me. Then they hop away in almost perfect synchronicity.

"Can you smell that fragrance?" Hildegard points at a yellow and pink coloured blossom. As I inhale the fragrance, joy spreads inside me. I start to smile and I take another deep breath in.

"A garden is healing. It transforms the great energies for those who look after it."

"Is that the reward for taking care of the plants?" I ask.

"It's a conversation," Hildgard smiles. "Looking after things, your devotion, the love you give the plants makes them flourish. Their response is to produce the medicine they give to you."

"How do they give me this medicine?"

"Their beauty, their fragrance, the atmosphere in a garden. All of that gives you joy, peace, love. The fruits the plants bear become your basic substances. You consume them. Their flavour opens your doors, in that way they have an effect inside you."

"Do you use the Garden Fields the same way?" I ask.

Hildegard is standing laughing in front of a white flower, the fragrance of which I can smell even from where I'm standing.

"Energy, everything is energy. Information is energy. The Garden Fields and the plants transform energy into the exact light frequencies an emoti needs. When an emoti takes care of the plants, they adapt to that frequency. The energy heals the resistances that might have got mixed in along the way."

I look at her confused. Hildegard's laugh is contagious. I let out a sigh of relief. "And that heals illnesses?" I ask.

"Indeed. The vital energy rebalances all the other imbalances that could form around the emoti."

"And what's the problem with the resistances?"

"They prevent the emoti from acting with light. Each emoti is created for a very specific purpose. Each has its own unique frequency, with which it serves the inner universe. Resistances are dark fields of energy. They envelop an emoti like a cloak. That hinders their deeds of light."

"Where do these resistances come from?"

"Being under stress or great pain – a resistance is initially there to protect an emoti. When the stress and the pain are over, it has to be actively dissolved. If it's left there for too long, it starts to act only in order to preserve itself. It uses the emoti's energy for that, weakens it, changes it."

The path in the labyrinth seems to be longer than I thought. We stop speaking and I try to understand the problem with the resistances. A cloak that first covers the emoti to protect it and then starts to exploit it? I imagine an old tree covered in ivy. How do you get rid of ivy? Cut it off?

"No," Hildgeard answers gently. "The emoti has to intensify their original energy – their light frequency. They have to get stronger in their deeds of light."

I must have a pretty dumb look on my face, because Hildegard starts laughing so loud that even the flowers around her start to dance. "I hear the frequency you're forming thoughts in. That's why I know what you're thinking without you saying anything."

I look at her skeptically. "Can everyone here do that?"

"No. It's a special gift."

I breathe a sigh of relief.

"Your thoughts are nothing but energy. They have frequencies too, just like we do here. I think that's how you listen to the radio out there."

I recall what Pedi said: I don't have to understand everything straight away. It makes me feel a lot more relaxed.

"I heard you're here because you want to know more about Ben too."

In a way, yes. I look at Dale, who's standing tall and motionless just outside the labyrinth, waiting.

"Resistances have no interest in taking care of the gardens. That would only weaken them. Emotis with powerful... resistances compensate for what they do in other ways. Extremes and basic substances cause the immediate effects of intoxication."

"Like smoking and alcohol?"

"Excessive sport, sex, the intoxication of success. It can all be cultivated by the resistances as replacement energy."

"Is that what happens in an addiction?"

"Only if a pattern of behaviour has been established alongside the intoxication. Then it's easy for the resistance to get the emoti to do something."

"Why does the Office tolerate it?"

"The emotis just submit an extra invoice after their work. That forces the Office to do something to avoid imbalances. As you know equilibrium is the fundamental aim here and everywhere, with you as well, in the world of form."

I look at a flower, around which another flower has wound itself. It's supporting it. And making it dependent, I suddenly realise. A deceitful system. Angrily, I try to rip off the climbing plant, then the stem of the other flower snaps in the middle and sinks to the ground. "Oh no!" I exclaim.

"Transformation has a chance if you strengthen what is light. Trust the natural order, trust strength and balance.

If you fight the darkness, the best you can hope is that both die."

"Ben has a big resistance that has completely merged with him. Everything he does is against the Garden Fields, against his own light side. The resistance makes him do it. It's sad to see."

Miss Intuition strokes a pink flower. "That's love too," she says quietly to herself.

"Can't anyone do anything?" I ask.

"*Anyone* can't do much, but *you* can," she says emphatically.

"Yeah, the detective already kind of told me that. I'm not sure if it's really true."

"Love can overcome everything," she says suddenly. "Your love."

What's she talking about? How can someone welcome behaviour like that, accept it, or even think it's good? It makes absolutely no sense.

"The very opposite, it makes sense to everyone, because it melts away walls." Hildegard looks at me lovingly, as if it were the most obvious thing in the world to answer my thoughts. So she knows everything. How can I argue with that? Just thinking nothing definitely doesn't work.

"And how exactly is that supposed to work? Should I challenge the Glutton to a duel? Should I convince him to run Section II properly or should I guard the entrance?"

"It sounds like you're ready for a fight. But that will only strengthen his resistance, give it energy."

"What? If I want to stop him, then I'm strengthening the resistance?"

"You have to think of the resistance as a false advisor, who keeps his master's will under control using his sorcery. This advisor learns more in each conflict and that way finds even better defence strategies."

"It sounds like a war," I observe with frustration.

"The war supplies the resistance, the false advisor with energy. He needs the enemy, his opponents, to get active, get energy. Your affection, acceptance and love make the fight impossible, they take away every resistance's opponent."

"Brilliant, then you have the solution: no one fights against him and everything will be fine," I assert with relief.

My willpower, a pool of transformation

We've arrived back to the start of the labyrinth. The detective has overheard my last comment and says decisively: "Only your strength, your willpower and your love can break the Glutton's power. The first impulse has to come from you, the first step of transformation."

"My willpower, the first step," I repeat, pensively. What is my willpower? I look at Hildegard questioningly.

"The Well of Transformation."

"The emotis go there to neutralise their alignment," Dale explains. "Their frequency, but not their structure is deleted. Then the emoti is available for new jobs afterwards."

Miss Intuition laughs. "Dale, always following the path of logic."

Dale suddenly looks very unsure; I know that feeling all too well. Hildegard lovingly puts a hand on his shoulder, which doesn't make things any better.

"It's a place," she says. "But most importantly, it's a connection to a great force, to the source, to God. It's meekness of the heart and destruction at the same time. The centre is neutral, harmonious, soft and gentle. But you will encounter the extremes there. The heat of fire and ice cold. You will only find the centre after you have experienced the outer extremes."

"Why is that?"

"Trans-form, it's getting-behind-the-form, overcoming the form if you like," Dale explains, full of enthusiasm.

"You can feel when this centre touches you, when you're ready for the depth, the emptiness that is underneath every form. You'll feel it," she says, then turns around and waves goodbye.

The detective and I stand at the edge of the labyrinth and watch her go.

"And the Glutton needs to take a dip in this Well of Transformation?" I ask to make sure I understand.

"That's the only chance he has of changing."

"The Well of Transformation, how will I find this place?"

The detective gives me a very precise description. Then, despite the risk that Hildegard might be listening, I say: "I need to think about it."

Dale and I are in complete agreement on this point. He takes a bow without another word and strides away at a brisk pace.

CHAPTER 15

What Have I Got to Lose?

*Recognising that the grass is green
and finding yourself*

I find myself drawn to the fragrant meadows the kangaroo led us across at the start. On the way, fragments of an excited conversation reach my ear.

"Of course he ignored it. What else would he do?"

"The poor guy..."

"Him in action, that would be..."

"Then you wouldn't get any cake."

"Re-ally? No-o-o, I'm sure there'd still be yummy cake then."

"One piece twice a week, that would be it."

"Su-re-ly not. And even if, it'd still be better than the horrible stuff I get now."

I look over the bushes. Suddenly I hear the voices on the other side of the path. Still nothing. Then in a little hollow, I see two pointy ears moving back and forth. The kangaroo in the hammock.

There's a stout, slightly chubby looking emoti sitting on a rock. His red velvet cloak covers most of his small shape.

"Hey Tom, how are you?" The kangaroo lifts a paw. I nod to him, but can't help looking back at the other guy's headgear several times.

"This is the Cake King," the kangaroo informs me. The Cake King then stands up and introduces himself a little clumsily.

"A cake king?"

"Does it surprise you?" the kangaroo asks and gives himself a big push with his tail, which causes the hammock to spit him out onto the ground. He gives himself a shake and carefully climbs back into the netting.

"What were you talking about just now?"

"About how the Gourmet's doing now," the Cake King answers and sighs loudly. "The Glutton threw him o-u-t this morning. I think the Gourmet's great and now he's gone."

"What?"

His crown slips forward and backwards on his head gently as the Cake King nods in affirmation.

"Why is the Glutton back in Section II?"

"Did you think he'd just give up, because you said that once?" the kangaroo asks, laughing. "You're gonna have to come up with something else."

"Pl-ea-se help us," pleads the Cake King.

"How? I have no idea how you work."

"I always go to the Guardian if I want to know something," says the kangaroo.

"The last time you didn't understand a word of what the Guardian said to you," says the Cake King.

"Tattletale," hisses the kangaroo.

"H-e-l-p us please. I really like the Gourmet."

I take a deep breath. The Garden Fields catch my eye. "I don't know…"

There's a rustle from one of the dry bushes, when the Cake King sits back down on his rock. There's a large sandy field behind him full of these skeletal plants.

"What am I supposed to do?" I ask, without really expecting an answer. Even though the kangaroo is acting cold, they both seem sad – and just as clueless about what to do as I am.

I continue, cross over to the meadow. I sit down in the tall grass, rest my head on my knees. Tears run over my arms and disappear into the criss-crossing green of the blades of grass.

Out of nowhere, I remember my last food binge: I open the fridge. As if I'm in a trance, I take out cheese, mayo, chili sauce. Then some bread, two slices, then two more. The leftover pasta from the day before, warm it up quickly. Some of it is stuck to the pot, some of it is cold – I don't care. Beer, YouTube, forgetting, not having to think, not having to feel. Just forget everything.

Nuts, crisps, just stuff them in, in, in.

It's never been so clear to me, so conscious, as it is now. It's the Glutton, his resistance is my hiding, my running away, my not wanting to feel. In this other state of being full and dull, nothing matters, everything is bearable, for a short while. As long as no one knows about it. The secret meetings, like PR said yesterday? The Free Radicals, the Glutton. They keep taking me over, having their food orgies, leaving their junk behind. It doesn't matter how my body deals with it, what it looks like afterwards, how it feels. It doesn't matter how much they're all suffering in my inner universe.

I feel dizzy. Everything is spinning. All that keeps running through my head is "why?" Why does it keep happening? Fear of being alone. Was that what caused my last food binge? Fear that Manú might reject me, that I could lose her? Is that the fear that activates the Glutton and pushes me into this binge eating?

The realisations are pounding down on me like a heavy rain. Buckets of realisations. Tears. Lots of tears. My stomach suddenly feels as heavy as stone. My body is screaming, it wants to be heard. I scream to let out the rage, the desperation. My voice cracks.

I stop for a moment, out of breath. The stones start to move in my stomach again. The heat rises inside me. I'm breathing fast. Suddenly I remember the gym-class situation from school again. I close my eyes; the whole of class 5c is standing in front of me. The high bar in the sports hall. I'm standing in front of it getting bigger and bigger: "No. No, not you," I scream. "Get out of here. Out!" I push Kevin, hard. He suddenly gets a taste of fear and runs out of the sports hall. The gym teacher's laugh gets stuck in his throat. It's quiet for a moment in the hall. Then I hear applause. I hear the clapping really clearly. The whole class is cheering. I look briefly at the others. Even the gym teacher gives me a nod of recognition. Then I get back in line; the others make space to accommodate me.

I open my eyes. I catch a few drops that fall from my chin. Tears, releasing the pain from my body. This pain, in the end, it's energy, that's all. It's all just energy.

Screaming, just energy.

A smile, just energy.

And my fear that activates the Glutton, what is that? I close my eyes again and see clouds, big and threatening. They seem real from a distance, but the closer I come, the more they dissolve, retreat, even disappear. Everything yields. A wall made of nothing? Then everything else along with the nothing is the ONE that appears in the form of many. Tears, screaming, laughter and fear.

For the first time, it's clear to me that fear doesn't need to direct my life. And yet it's there every day, can be seen everywhere, just like the clouds.

What are clouds? They're water that comes from the source of springs, protected underneath rock. The water gives me life, gives me strength – for tears, screams and my laughter.

The next breath opens thousands of flowers, which caress my body. Slowly, I lift my head, open my eyes. What was that? Where am I? My arms – as light as a feather. My stomach? The stones are gone. Even my bulging belly seems to be gone. I carefully lift my shoulders, make some circles with my head. One more breath. As if being controlled by a strange force, I stand up again, almost without any of my own effort. I look down at my body. Yes, somehow it's beautiful. I look over to the Factory. "I'll help you. Whatever happens, I'll help you."

CHAPTER 16

Being the Change

Leap of faith

I head towards the Factory with a firm step. When I get there, I stop in front of the gate to Section II. I take a deep breath, then I push it open and go in.

"Hello?" Is there really no one here? I can't believe that. I cross the first Factory floor carefully. It smells musty. In the corner there's a pile of containers leaking a dark, thick substance.

The second door I find seems locked, but I hear voices behind a third.

"This will all be torn down. We need space," someone screeches, sounding annoyed.

My hand rests motionless on the cold door handle for a moment.

"Tomorrow, the next delivery, where should we put it?"

It must be about a new delivery of basic substances. I feel the pressure on the door handle, before it slowly yields. The screeching voice stops. There's no going back now. The door opens noisily. I close my eyes, hear my heart thumping. Clouds of fear. I just have to go in. Determined, I take the next step.

The Glutton and the Tiger are standing in the corner of the room with two other emotis.

"Where's the Gourmet?" I ask.

The Glutton laughs out loud, shakes his head.

"I want to talk to you! Alone!"

The Glutton – or Ben, yes Ben is better – continues laughing artificially.

"Please," I add meekly.

The four of them whisper briefly to each other, then the two other emotis leave with the Tiger and Ben comes towards me. Pinkie gives a short bark. Only the tips of his ears are peeking out of the bag, which bangs against Ben's chest with every step.

"Why?" I ask.

"What, why? This is my job. I built all of this up, I did. If the Gourmet still had a say, we'd live in a broom cupboard and give every piece of bread a name. We need structure, we need to think big!"

"Do we need the dry bushes and the vital energy disappearing from the Garden Fields too?"

"That's not my fault..."

"Oh, it's not?"

"What can I do about the heat drying everything out?"

"And the junk?" The open door reveals the sight of the containers, whose stink wafts all the way to where we are.

"If the Gourmet would do his job properly, we wouldn't be here."

"It won't lead to anything." What did Hildegard say? Acceptance and love will melt the walls. I'll worry about the love later. "Come on, let's go outside."

"Why? I'm busy."

"Please." Unwilling, he follows me to the exit, mumbling something incomprehensible. Pinkie looks out of his bag curiously. He's actually quite cute, the little guy.

On the way to the Garden Fields

"How did you end up with this job?"

"This place was a mess and I had time."

"What do you mean?"

"The selection of the basic substances was a disaster. Nothing was good enough. Complaints from the world of form were piling up. And it was always the same here. I took the basic substances that were offered to us and ordered them regularly. Then the complaints soon stopped."

"And what was your job before that?" I change the subject.

He doesn't answer.

"What makes you so angry about the Gourmet?"

"He always thinks he knows better. If I didn't have all this responsibility, I could talk as much as he does too."

"Is the responsibility for all of the basic substances too much for you?" I ask this question more quietly, almost as if I'm asking myself.

"I taught myself all of this. I built it up from nothing. Now it's all wrong? I don't know anything, right! Am I too stupid for it or something?"

"No, not too stupid. Maybe you're doing something you just don't enjoy anymore?"

"Ha. How would you know?"

"There are piles of junk all over the place. More and more emotis are suffering because of it. And you? You don't really seem happy either." The Glutton laughs extremely loudly.

"All of this is harming my inner universe and in the last few years, it's caused me a lot of pain in my life out there."

"So I'm to blame for everything. I'm too stupid for my job! Stupid, stupid! Then kill me. Then at least you'll be rid of me, if I'm only a nuisance, if I do everything wrong. I'm just an idiot!"

"Well, you are behaving like one!" Angrily, I look away, take a deep breath in. How can I accept this, how am I supposed to accept THIS GUY? My stomach is doing somersaults. The stones are back. I look straight into his face. "Stop all this! You can't go on like this – no way. Things have changed."

Ben is almost foaming at the mouth with rage. But at the same time, I think I see something like sadness in his eyes.

"You want to get rid of me. I was good enough until now. Now I have to go. You're... Do you like tormenting me like this?"

"No one wants to torment you." I try to stay calm, but my heart is beating fast.

"You have no idea what happens here…"

"But I do know that you'll ruin us all! I can't let that happen!" I step closer to him. He takes a step back. "You don't give a crap if the others are suffering. Your hatred makes you only think about yourself." My body is trembling. I take two deep breaths. Some cold water would be good right now. "Listen, Ben, I relieve you of all your duties."

He laughs out loud again. "What did you say?" He pretends as if he didn't hear me properly.

"You are no longer responsible for Section II, effective immediately. And you…"

"You can't tell me what to do…"

"And you're not allowed to enter the Factory," I speak over him.

There's a brief pause. I calm down a bit.

"You have to find your purpose again. We'll help you find your purpose again." This idea makes me happy and for a moment the rage subsides. "You'll find your place again. Trust me." I'm standing very close to him, I feel his despair and his fear.

"You don't want this either. Whoever pushed you in here, it's not your destiny, it was never what you were meant to do. It was always the Gourmet's. He finds it easy to manage Section II. He's passionate about all this, he senses the strength in the basic substances. He knows how things work. You had to manage to get by without that depth of knowledge and the connection. But it's over now."

Ben starts to breathe heavily, starts to cry, wailing like

a cat, awful. Standing beside him feels like the repulsion between two magnets. So much for acceptance. But I hold my ground. "You're relieved of all your duties." For a moment I'm able to feel his pain. His whimpering and at the same time his resistance: "It's not your place to decide!"

I take him in my arms. He resists, pulls back and pushes me away. "Stop it!"

I go towards him again. I take him in my arms again. I repeat the same words.

"I hate you."

"I know."

"How can you do this to me?"

I say nothing and try my best to ignore my repulsion towards him, my disgust.

"I always did my best." His words sound almost meek now.

"I never really gave you enough respect," I admit.

"I want to be worth something too," he says, surprisingly.

"You are worth something. And you can show us that, with your true skills you can prove that."

"How?"

"Take some time for yourself, for your transformation." I look at him hopefully. There's a war going on inside him, I can see that clearly. He seems smaller now, much smaller. We sit down together, exhausted, side by side on his garden field, which is basically a desert. We don't know what to say and maybe we don't have the strength to go on shouting at each other. It's quiet now. I would really like to move away from him now. It feels sticky, repulsive, disgusting and yet like it belongs to me. I'm his key to freedom. My willpower is his light, which might blind a little at the start. I have to help him, no matter what that feels like. I will give him my complete attention from now on. The only thing is: he won't continue his job in the Factory, I have to prevent that.

"What did you do before you came to the Factory?" I ask.

"I don't know. Do you?"

"We have to find out."

"It's pointless."

"I don't think so," I say with determination and jump up. "You're going to help me find out." I pull him up too. Once again, I feel a little surge of happiness. Ben says nothing and Pinkie looks out of his handbag cautiously.

Unexpectedly, but with determination too, Ben starts walking. Does he know more than he's saying? I like the idea that he does. "We have a mission," I say exhilarated. "Where are we going?"

"To the Factory, where else? I'm already really late."

"Stop!" I block his path. "That's over. You're not going back."

"Are you going to stop me?"

"I will," I say calmly. "Come with me."

Things get heated again. Once again, he screams about how he's worth nothing. And yet he's too scared to keep going. Once again, I find it very hard to give him recognition. I feel his anger everywhere and yet he's only standing in front of me with it. His anger, his despair – are they a part of me? And yet not me? Always in that one place but never everywhere? I'm not Ben, I'm just close to him. If I fight against him, then the fight turns against me. Only my willpower, my desire to change can bring transformation for him.

I try to stick to this attitude and suddenly he's following me, on through the Garden Fields and the many dry bushes.

"How do you use these bushes?" I ask.

"How should I use them?"

"Aren't these plants supposed to have flowers and help you with your deeds of light?"

"All crap!" He hits a bush with contempt, then himself. I realise how little he knows about what could be possible if he was operating on full strength. If he could just only use the strength from the gardens again.

I look at him. I almost manage a smile. He brings a few branches back in order, pulls a few others off and at the same time tries to replant them. Kneeling, he slides to the next bush. I stop, put my hand on his shoulder. He stops, jerks back halfheartedly. I hold my ground. He lets it happen. We look at his garden field: a desert of despair, lifeless forms.

"Let's begin," I say quietly.

"With what?"

"Creating a transformation?"

"What good will that do?" This ignorance unleashes a new wave of anger inside me.

At the same time I see emotis gathering at the edge of some of the Garden Fields. They're watching us. A short time later, they appear again at the other end of the Garden Fields. I recognise Con and the kangaroo. I look left and right, start breathing faster. More and more of them are gathering. What now?

"What do they want here? Get lost!" he shouts over.

I stand there, alone. My only chance is my willpower, my determination to change. And Ben's standing there. I quickly look over to the others.

It has never been so clear to me: the moment you step out to face that creature, you step out alone.

I look at the others one more time, then I go over to Ben. In a swift move, I take the frightened Pinkie out of the handbag and put him carefully on the ground. He races around the dried out bushes, overjoyed, squeaking, leaping around like a lamb in spring.

"What are you doing?" Ben tries to catch him again, but Pinkie has already run off to the next bush. I hold Ben back. "Look how happy he is. Watch him. How wonderful."

Ben falls silent. I start to hum quietly. It turns into a melody, repeating, always the same.

When he tries to retreat again, I resolutely and tightly hold onto him. I stand in front of him, very close. "Pinkie doesn't need the bag anymore."

"What are you talking about? Of course he needs it, when we're in the Factory. Do you want him to get killed?" Ben grips the bag tightly. I reach for it. Like putting a saddle on a wild horse for the first time, Ben keeps ducking out of the way of my hand. Then I manage to grab one handle of the bag. I'm faced with his opposition, his screaming, naked fear. Then I manage to get the second handle and Pinkie's house falls onto the ground. The little guy just looks up briefly at the scene, until a cheeky leaf dances past him. He immediately starts chasing it and disappears.

"Look at the fun he's having." Ben looks to where he's just disappeared. Then he tries to take the bag back, but I manage to keep hold of it.

"Your job is finished," I declare loudly. "Pinkie doesn't need the bag anymore."

Ben won't give up, he clamours and screams, throws himself onto the ground. He screams and screams and screams.

I set fire to one of the dry bushes and within a flash it's up in flames. The bag sails into the fire in a high arc. Ben is immediately on his feet to try to rescue the bag. With all my strength, I try to hold him back. The burning bush is now fully ablaze and with it the bag. Its pink colour quickly fades. In a moment of inattentiveness, Ben manages to grab the bag and pulls at it forcefully. I pull him back. The bag flies up into the air and falls onto another bush, which catches fire straight away. It quickly spreads to other bushes. It gets hotter and brighter and hotter. We have to retreat to the verdant and damp herb meadow, where the flames can't catch. Soon Ben's entire garden field is in flames. Ben is exhausted; despairing and very quiet, he collapses into a ball on the meadow.

The hordes of spectators start to move, to put out the flames. Bucket after bucket of clear water is poured onto the flames, which, hissing, turn into damp steam. They look happy, not appalled. I hear laughter, not screams. They dance and help each other to dissolve the old and make space for the new. The water moistens the whole universe and the dryness visibly starts to recede. It feels warm and damp. In the turmoil, I hear voices calling out: "The weather's changing, the weather's changing." It's like a celebration, a celebration of making space for the new.

Ben is sitting in the grass at a bit of a distance to the action. I hold him close to me. Tears flow. We don't say anything.

When the smoke finally clears, we look at the scorched, damp earth. Whatever wants to grow here, it now has the space to grow, there's enough of it.

I stand up, firmly pull Ben to his feet and gently lead him away from the meadow and the site of the fire. Apathetic and exhausted, he lets it happen, doesn't fight back. Pinkie is still running around in high spirits, barking at the flowers, throwing himself on his back and rubbing his fur on the ground.

We walk in the direction of the forest, towards the other gate. The wide road with its bright, white shimmer will help to orientate me, that's what the detective said.

CHAPTER 17

In the Well of Transformation

Finding new hope

This part of the inner universe proves foreign to me. We must be close to the gate, but no one seems to have heard of it. Take a right, then somewhere here... something round should appear. Ben, behind me, is looking at the ground. He seems small and slim, takes no notice of me looking at him. Then he stops. Something seems to be happening inside him. He bends down, picks a flower and sticks it in his buttonhole. Is that a smile? Then he kneels down onto the ground, laying out leaves and branches in a beautiful pattern, three stones, and another flower.

"Wow. What's that?"

"Nothing special. I used to do that quite a lot. Just like that."

"What did you used to do?" I hunker down beside him.

He looks down at the arrangement. "Things like this. With the food."

"Was that your purpose? Think about it. Do you remember anything else?"

"No, nothing. Doesn't matter. I don't know." In one swoop, he suddenly sweeps his hand through his artwork. He stands up, picks up a heavy stone and...

"Ben! No! You're an artist, a really good one."

Ben freezes. I turn around. Paul Relations is standing behind us, Mr PR.

"What do you want here? Get lost!"

"Ben. Please listen to me."

I carefully take the stone out of Ben's hands and stand aside.

"Listen to me," says Paul.

"What else do you want from me? Everything's...."

"It wasn't your fault. It was chaos back then. No one really knew what happened."

"And then I was the scapegoat. Was simple. He doesn't notice anything anyway."

"No, it wasn't like that."

"Why didn't you help me then?" Ben asks his brother. "You just went into public relations, had a great new job. How could you just ignore my situation?"

"Pushing you away. Letting it happen, it was so wrong. I wish I had done more for you. No one saw it coming. The rejection, no one knew how to handle it."

I'm listening, quiet as a mouse. Here, inside me, I'm listening. These two brothers in front of me, the sports issue, the rejection, all one. And yet there are still big gaps.

"Why?" I interrupt.

They both look at me. Then Ben looks at the ground. Paul is searching for the right words. He scratches his head, looks away, then at me. I look straight back at him, waiting for answers.

"We set up the stage back then."

"The stage? What stage?"

"Everything that has to do with interacting with the outer world happens on this stage. Since then no one really can see into the inner universe."

"Is it a kind of mask?"

"A theatre play with masks, costumes, drama. We perform life."

"Perform life?" I repeat, talking to myself. But it doesn't seem any more believable.

"Then everything I present to the outside is just an illusion?"

"Not only. Often the performance almost matches what's really going on. But we always keep control of what gets broadcast out and especially how it gets broadcast."

We stop talking for a moment. I heard everything he just said. It's hot here all of a sudden. My life, an illusion? I have to sit down on the closest rock.

"And," my voice is hoarse, "what does that..."

I look over at Ben, who speaks, lost in his thoughts. "I guess I just didn't fit in."

"You didn't want to take this path," Paul adds.

"But it's not right, fooling everyone. I couldn't do it. Someone had to maintain the beautiful things."

"Your fearless and open way of dealing with the world

of things put the whole stage project in danger. I couldn't do anything. The others were in agreement that you had to end the art of joy."

"What's that? Art of joy?" I look at both of them inquisitively.

"Ben turned everything into art," Paul says hesitantly. "Everyone has a plate full of food. His looks like a piece of art a few minutes later. But especially in the Garden Fields." He looks over to Ben. He nods suddenly.

"Yes, the mini-paradise."

"He even turned weeds into works of art. That's how he spread joy throughout the inner universe, for all of us."

I shake my head in astonishment. "And that didn't fit in with the stage project?" I get up, pace to and fro for a minute, and then sit down again. "Why?"

"This innocent joy, this carefree nature, made us vulnerable – open to attack. When it sweats, it sweats. When it's hungry, it eats, when it's sad, it cries. That's how that disaster in gym class happened in the first place. We had nothing to fight back with. Absolutely nothing. Nothing to defend ourselves. With that openness and those honest feelings, we made ourselves a laughing stock for everyone," Paul says in defence of those events. I look at both of them speechless. A thought forms through the fog in my mind.

Hazily, I remember a present I put in that guy Kevin's backpack before gym class. What was it again?

"It's all over. All in the past," says Ben. "We can't get it back."

"I don't agree," I say, jump up and look from one to the other. They really are brothers. Crazy.

"I'll be back in a minute," I say and go a bit further into the forest. It must be here somewhere. The detective described it exactly. Everything seems right, I just can't find the strange entrance...

Then all of a sudden I see an oval opening parting the undergrowth. Completely camouflaged by its surroundings, a door seems to block the oval entrance.

"I found it," I shout. "Ben, I found it." My heart is thumping against my chest like mad. Stay calm, stay calm.

Startled, he looks up. "Come here!"

Paul stands up and helps Ben up too. "Let's start over."

They look at each other for a moment, hug each other a bit awkwardly, then I pull Ben away.

We go to this oval entrance in the forest. Clouds of fear begin to gather. I pass through them just like that. What a new experience.

When we've arrived at the entrance, I look at Ben. "Us two, me and you, we're going to go in there now and let it happen."

"What have I got to lose?"

I nod at him and open the door. We go in. The lock clicks behind us. Something starts to move, gently pulling me along a path, which appears in the blue shimmer.

Surrender

My body feels like it's being guided, floating, towards a
nothing. A quiet doubt arises in me. It seems to ask me:
Do I really want this? A transformation? Are you ready?

Oh yes, I am. I could hardly feel any more ready, after
everything that's happened.

In the very same moment, a strange force lifts me up
and lays me gently down on the ground. It becomes clear
to me that I've lost control of my body. I can't open my
eyes. Arms and legs motionless. As heavy as lead, I melt
down into the undergrowth. A laugh fills me. And tears.

I'm enveloped by a warm rain.
The link to my body dissolves.
I feel the fear start to spread.
Yet my body remains, I live,
And now I'm floating in the light.
I feel safe and held, still.

Then sunlight shining upon me.
Why does it all seem so familiar?
The heat burns, yet does not harm me.
It burns away my thoughts,
Bushes that did not resist the flames.
In the black earth, I see my face.

A gust of strong wind,
Followed closely by a storm.

All that was holding on now lets go.
Old worries, hesitation must be gone,
It will no longer serve in what's to come.
What is old screams out in despair.

Now I am gripped by an icy cold,
Crystals twinkle, roughly formed.
My wildest thoughts freeze in the frost,
The thoughts that restlessly pursue me,
And prevent me from embracing loving beauty,
Which in fact protects me, dismantles barriers.

And now? A quiet rumbling,
Then I hear it beating louder.
A bolt of thunder penetrates my being.
Yet I feel as if I'm being carried.
Flashes of lightning, strong and bright.
The end is almost in sight!

But no, the forcefield dissipates
The air vibrates with sound.
How magical this melody.
I hear love singing of love.
It seems I myself vibrate in these sounds,
As I rotate here in complete harmony.

Then it becomes quiet and lovely.
Crystal white light radiates peacefully.
This moment wants to show me now.

I let it happen; I surrender myself.
Recognise myself as I am.
I've found my place here, I want to stay.

It's quiet for a moment. Then I feel some drops and with the warm rain the cycle begins again from the start. I take this journey many times, always the same. Each time I can feel more, hear more, see more, smell more and taste more. A curiosity grows in me and I ask myself: What else? What else can I discover? Only now I notice a forking path – one path leads inwards, one outwards. Who will decide which path I will take?

Then I am drawn further inwards, further towards the centre of the circle.

The seventh chamber

Suddenly, a space opens up before me that feels very different. Still floating, I slowly sink down towards a form. Is that my body? Is this my shell waiting for the return of its life? As I approach, the doubt whether I want to go in there grows, but the feeling of gravitation gets stronger, pulling me down to the ground. Very slowly this shell merges with the life force. With me. How lovely that sounds. With me. This heavy shell and this lightness, two things wanting to occupy one place. But then, a sudden jerk and the two become one.

Am I lying down, sitting, or standing? Fingers? Can be

moved. Toes? So can they. I stretch, breathe, hum away to myself. Then I move my arms, my legs and, like a rabbit, my nose. Is this some body moving – or is it my body? I pinch my upper arm. Ouch!

The eyes? Are a bit sticky. I only manage to open them slowly. In slow motion, I pick myself up. This place, bright from the greenish shimmer. It feels wonderful. There, a dark patch. It's moving, even speaking. I know the voice.

Slowly, the image comes into focus. Is that the Guardian coming towards me?

"A transformation has taken place. Structures altered, new forms created. Now integration, discovering what newness wants to reveal itself."

He looks at me with loving kindness: *"Old thinking, old behaviour too will knock upon the door. Do not open the door anymore, even if I feel I should."*

The Guardian looks at me softly. A friendly face. We're standing facing each other. I'm still trying to get my bearings.

"Where's Ben?" I ask finally.

"Forty days, should provide the help, to break the resistances so strong. In the cycle of transformation, he still is."

"And me? What am I doing here?"

He smiles. *"Six chambers, you passed through again and again. Until into full surrender you let go. Wanting dissolved, liberated you were led on, until you fell into this chamber, last step."*

"Didn't this wanting not lead me exactly here, to this place of transformation?"

"Determination to love, not willpower from fear or anger, for you opens the door to transformation."

Nodding, I look at him. His words are slowly revealing their meaning and depth to me. So it was surrender, which I was able to allow earlier with the Glutton, which led me to find the door to the Well of Transformation. Transformation begins with letting go of the old. Acceptance, letting go. I have to laugh. Can it be that simple? You have to first clear off the table before you can put something new on it?

"What's going to happen in this chamber now? Is this also part of the transformation?" I ask the Guardian. I look at him. It's nice to have this companion with me: in my dreams, on the shamanic journeys, on the way to the inner universe and now here. He's always there when I let things happen.

"An end is coming. You will leave in this form the world in energies now. This journey you will end with strength, energy now is filling itself in your body."

The Guardian smiles. I breathe and once again I let happen what should happen.

An intense force takes hold of me. Almost electrified, everything in me is vibrating. Is it lifting me up, am I separating from my body again? No, it feels different. I feel the connection, the energy surging through my body.

This force surges through me several times, until I unexpectedly find myself standing at the edge of the herb meadow.

The vibration is gone. So is the Guardian. My body feels completely calm. I look around. Something's moving over there. "Manú?"

"There you are," she says.

Still in slow motion, I walk towards her. "How did you get here?" I ask.

"The Guardian led me here. First, he explained it to me. But you know what his explanations are like. Then he showed me; that was simple."

I smile at her lovingly. "You are…"

"Yes?"

"…a wonderful person."

Then I take her in my arms. "If only you knew…"

"I know."

"You know?"

She nods. "The others do too. You did a lot. They're so happy, so grateful. You'll see."

Not far from us, some emotis are busy putting out little fires.

New guidance

We go over to them and they cheer as they see us coming. More and more arrive. Applause. Louder and louder. Soon a big crowd is standing all around us. The detective nods to me with appreciation from among the throng.

"It's done."

"Not quite yet," I say.

I look for the Gourmet and ask him to come with me.

"My dear Gourmet. Are you ready to take on your old job again?"

He nods. "I think so."

"I trust you completely. Bring joy back into the Factory. Let's find the best basic substances."

He stands up a little taller, looks out into the crowd, positively beaming.

"Section II has its old management again – the Gourmet is back!" I shout.

Cheering. I put my hand on his shoulder. Then we hug. He looks at me, clearly moved. His shining eyes express happiness and gratitude.

I beckon the Cake King and the Tiger over to us.

"There's new work for you to do. We're gonna need your strength and joy, for the Factory. For the change that's coming. For the inner universe."

The two of them look at me. The Cake King comes to stand at my side. "I'm ready!" The applause makes him beam too. His crown is dancing on his head.

The Tiger's tail is dancing like a snake too. He stands up, sits down, stands up.

"Everything's going to be different. Are you ready?"

The Cake King looks over at him. "Come on. We can do it."

The Tiger looks into the crowd, then to the Factory, stands up, circles around us and then lets out a loud growl and sits down beside the Cake King.

We all look at each other, nod, and wave to the crowd. What a feeling, this happiness gushing at us from them. How wonderful. How alive. How beautiful!

A *farewell*

The time to say goodbye is nearing and the Guardian is preparing to bring us to the gate. Con and Pedi say farewell to us in their usual formal way. The White Knight, the politician, the detective all wish us well. Miss Intuition sends over a waft of the fragrance of roses, Pinkie and the Terrier bark excitedly and the kangaroo wraps his short arms around Manú and me. "Have a good journey," he says with an audible gulp.

Somewhere at the back, someone is hectically gathering up in pieces of notepaper from the ground. I take a last look at everyone. My new family. My new self – a we.

Following the Guardian down the main road, we finally set off on our way to the entrance gate. "I'm still thinking about one question," I say. "Why do I see you and my inner universe so clearly?"

"Clairvoyant talents, perhaps?" wonders Manú, elated.

The Guardian stops in his tracks, turns around to face us.

"*Meaning in things embeds. The energy draws bridges with colours, we are connected through light and sound and fragrance at the same time. Symbols the world explains to us, giving the gift of discernment and storing knowledge until to experience we desire. The power of form is stored in our thoughts and here is created what became known elsewhere.*"

We have arrived at the gate. I remember the fright I got

when I looked into the kangaroo's ears when we arrived and smirk. With one last bow, the Guardian allows us to pass through.

"*Now it is time to let go of the said-felt-heard that comes from the centre of others. Then new things will form, where once old doubts resided.*"

CHAPTER 18

And then...?

A yellow Mini rolls home

Back at the stones, we follow the narrow path back along the lake.

"I saw you at the gate. What were you doing there?" I ask.

"I wanted to be alone. What I told you about my grandmother really upset me. I had the feeling I had to let go a bit more of something. Old thoughts, feelings – fears. I met the Guardian at the gate."

"I see."

"He took me to his garden field. I've never smelled anything like it. Never seen such beauty."

I smile at her, am happy for her, from the bottom of my heart. "That sounds wonderful."

"I sat there, I was able to give my feelings some space, my fears started to shift because of the fragrance and the peace there was there."

"Started to shift?" I ask.

"They transformed. Joy, suddenly I felt pure joy about the whole thing."

"Wow. You transformed in my inner world. How crazy is that!" Manú shrugs her shoulders.

"Then I suddenly saw the smoke and when more and more emotis were going there, I went with them. That's how I found you."

"You were at the dry fields?"

"And then you went off in the direction of the forest and the other gate. Someone said you were going to the Well of Transformation. I asked the Guardian about the path. He wanted to go there too and took me along."

"I met him in the Seventh Chamber," I say.

Manú smiles. "He didn't really want to talk about where he was going and suddenly he was gone."

We stop, look out over the lake. For quite a while, we just stand there like that. It's not easy to leave this view behind.

In the car, we look at our phones in astonishment. "Still Sunday or Sunday again?" Manú asks.

"Nothing can shock me now. It's just Sunday."

"Tom?"

I look at her.

"Could you bring the car back by yourself? I'd like to stay here for the night."

"Sure, no problem. Where are you going to stay?"

"Do you remember the little house, down by the lake?"

"A perfect place to rest after this – uh – journey."

"And what a journey it was. Your inner world is definitely not boring."

We look at each other for a long time. Then I take Manú in my arms. "Thanks."

"For what?"

"Just because and for..." Her lips stop me from continuing to speak.

Quite a while later, I finally finish the sentence: "...being there."

The yellow Mini rolls slowly along the road. A soft smile keeps creeping across my lips. There seems to be no gravity in my stomach. The tips of butterfly wings are tickling me there. It's dark and yet it seems so bright. I stop at a clearing, turn off the engine and get out of the car. The fresh forest air feels good. It's completely quiet. Only this endless current rushing inside me. Am I glowing or is it the moon? I shake my head and start to laugh again.

The moon makes the trees look like black lines. But the tips of the leaves are shining in the moonlight. Is that an owl whose cry I hear in the twilight? I can see a few faint stars above me. There'll be a new day tomorrow. And inside me? There's a new life.

THOUGHTS FROM THE AUTHOR

There are many paths towards a goal. At the same time, these paths symbolise a lack of purpose in the sense of non-goal. When your path reaches its highest fulfillment in every step, then you have arrived. Then you are at home. At the start maybe only for a second, then a few minutes, then longer and longer.

Writing this book may give the impression that I have seen and experienced something in the course of my journey, here on earth. But that doesn't protect me any more than any other human being from falling back again, into the unconscious, into sleep. To realise something, to awaken in one experience or another is wonderful. It reveals to me a little more of the miracle that is this earth and the universal forces behind the forms. Maybe it's a bit like pixels on a television screen. If enough pixels light up, you can see more of the picture. But the pixels can also go out again. That's how Eckhart Tolle once put it, and that's how I can most relate to awakening.

So at this point I would like to ask for you to be

tolerant with me, because I too am unconsciously on the move, again and again. I too fall asleep again and I too act unconsciously. We are all on this journey and we all make mistakes, good mistakes, because that is how we recognise ourselves when we look.

The emotis inside me are always quick to take over and act according to old patterns. These days I can laugh about it more often than I judge myself for it. Sometimes maybe we all just need to be human and act a bit egotistically. It is part of us and as such it is part of nature.

Best wishes,
Tom Millar

ABOUT THE AUTHORS

TOM MILLAR (36) is a professional hotel management consultant, lecturer and hotel certifications inspector. He lives in Berlin, where he began to deepen his interest in spirituality. He has travelled in Asia, where he learned about Buddhism and meditation in Thailand. At the same time, he is sceptical about the concept of yoga as it appears in the Western world.

Writing came into Tom's life by chance. He never thought about it before, but various circumstances led him to change his mind. That is why he is so thankful that he met Dirk and they got to co-create a first book – INNER UNIVERSE. Being an expert in communication methods didn't help much when it came to writing a story. But challenges are there to be overcome and this story is definitely worth sharing. Tom is eager to do so and so took a leap of faith.

DIRK BRÜCKNER (46) is familiar with writing from his scholarly work. This is his first novel, where he explores his spiritual interests. In his first book — on working as a travel guide — he already dealt with the idea of human interaction through observant self-awareness. An interest in self-development and yoga led Dirk to India, where he encountered Vedic teachings in ashrams and yoga schools. He was previously familiar with the teachings of Buddha, what a "spiritual path" can reveal, and why this must always intersect with personal growth. Now, with this book, Dirk puts his desire to bring people together with themselves and share spiritual wisdom in a simple manner down on paper.